KU-090-199

EDITION 1st

PRINT No. 80,000

COVER PTR Concise

The Marquis of Swayne is injured in
a carriage accident and is carried to
the house of the local physician. Here
he is nursed by Rowena, oldest of a
surprisingly beautiful family. The
Marquis learns that Doctor Winsford,
dedicated to his profession, is so
generous to his poorer patients that
his children suffer. He falls in love
with Rowena, and she with him, and
he offers her his protection.

How Rowena, horrified and
disillusioned by such a suggestion
fights against the Marquis's charm
and determination, how she tries to
defeat him in a battle of wills and
fails is told in this 199th book by
Barbara Cartland.

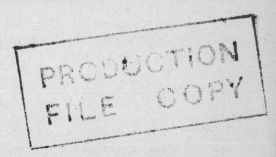

Also by Barbara Cartland

Books of Love, Life and Health
THE YOUTH SECRET
THE MAGIC OF HONEY
THE MAGIC OF HONEY COOK BOOK
THE FASCINATING FORTIES
MEN ARE WONDERFUL
FOOD FOR LOVE
LOVE, LIFE AND SEX
RECIPES FOR LOVERS

Historical Biography
THE OUTRAGEOUS QUEEN
THE PRIVATE LIFE OF CHARLES II
THE SCANDALOUS LIFE OF KING CAROL
METTERNICH
DIANE DE POITIERS

Romances
THE MAGNIFICENT MARRIAGE
THE KARMA OF LOVE
THE MASK OF LOVE
A SWORD TO THE HEART
BEWITCHED
THE IMPETUOUS DUCHESS
SHADOW OF SIN
THE GLITTERING LIGHTS
THE DEVIL IN LOVE
THE TEARS OF LOVE
A DREAM FROM THE NIGHT
NEVER LAUGH AT LOVE
THE PROUD PRINCESS
THE SECRET OF THE GLEN
THE HEART TRIUMPHANT
HUNGRY FOR LOVE
THE DISGRACEFUL DUKE
VOTE FOR LOVE

and published by Corgi Books

Barbara Cartland

A Duel with Destiny

CORGI BOOKS
A DIVISION OF TRANSWORLD PUBLISHERS LTD

A DUEL WITH DESTINY

A CORGI BOOK 0 552 10549 X

First publication in Great Britain

PRINTING HISTORY
Corgi edition published 1977

Corgi Books are published by
Transworld Publishers Ltd.,
Century House, 61–63 Uxbridge Road,
Ealing, London W5 5SA
Made and printed in Great Britain by
Cox & Wyman Ltd., London, Reading and Fakenham

Editor of:
The Common Problems by Ronald Cartland (with a preface by the Rt. Hon. The Earl of Selborne, P.C.)

Drama:
Blood Money
French Dressing

Philosophy:
Touch the Stars

Radio Operetta:
The Rose and the Violet (Music by Mark Lubbock)
performed in 1942.

Radio Plays:
The Caged Bird: An Episode in the Life of Elizabeth, Empress of Austria. Performed in 1957.

Verse:
Lines on Life and Love

AUTHOR'S NOTE

The fête given at Carlton House on August 1st, 1815, by the Prince Regent as a personal tribute to the Duke of Wellington is factual, as are the descriptions of the celebrations in the London Parks.

Genealogy no longer concerns itself exclusively with the lineage of the highly placed, but has an equal concern for all sorts and conditions of men. The Registration Act of 1836 made it compulsory in England to register births, marriages and deaths.

State records can be consulted at the Public Records Office in Chancery Lane, London where there are the historic documents such as the Domesday Book (1086–87) and Magna Carta (1215). In the United States of America interest in Genealogy goes back to the early days of British Settlement. The first families of Virginia constituted themselves a planter autocracy and used armorial bearings.

CHAPTER ONE

1815

Rowena heard the knocker on the front door and put down the sock she was darning.

It would be useless to expect old Mrs. Hanson to hear it in the kitchen. She was getting deafer every year and made it an excuse for not hearing the door or orders that she did not want to execute.

Rowena supposed it was one of her father's patients and thought that the knock sounded as if the caller was in a hurry; probably it was for a woman in labour, or for a worker on the adjacent farm who had been involved in an accident.

She crossed the small hall and opened the door, to stand astonished as she saw four men carrying a gate on which there was a recumbent figure.

"What has happened?" she asked.

"Doctor says as we're ter bring th' gent'man here," one of the men answered.

Rowena looked critically at the four-barred gate they had obviously taken off its hinges.

"You will not get that through the door," she said, "and certainly not up the stairs. You will have to carry him."

"That's wot oi told ye," one man said to another.

They all came from the village and Rowena knew them by name.

"What happened, Abe?" she asked the oldest of the four.

"Accident at th' cross-roads, Miss Rowena, a real nasty one, t'were!"

9

He and the other men were setting the gate down on the ground as he spoke and now Rowena looked at the figure lying on it and saw that it was in fact a gentleman resplendently dressed.

He wore an intricately-tied white cravat and the polish on his Hessian boots caught her attention before she realised how big he was and how tall he would be if he was standing.

"Oi says th' driver o' th' Stage-coach were drunk agin," one of the other men said.

"They causes more accidents then anyone else," a third chimed in.

"How many people were hurt?" Rowena asked.

"Only this gent'man," Abe replied. "Th' passengers on th' Stage-coach were real shook up, screamin' and a-cryin' they were, but th' Doctor's attendin' to 'em."

Rowena thought it was fortunate that her father had been there and remembered he had had a call to make in the village and then was going on to one of the out-lying farms.

This meant that he must have been near the cross-roads at the time of the accident.

The four men were lifting the gentleman off the gate. He was obviously very heavy, for they had to brace their muscles to take his weight. Now slowly they brought him into the house and started to climb the narrow stairway.

There was only one bed-chamber in the house that was not occupied, where Rowena knew they would have to put him.

It had been her mother's and was an attractive room with a bow-window overlooking the garden at the back.

She hurried ahead to pull up the blinds and turn down the sheets.

The bed was always made, for this was by no means the first time her father had used it for one of his patients.

The last time it had been occupied she remembered it was by a woman traveller who had slipped one frosty night and broken her leg.

She had been with them for nearly three weeks and a terrible trouble she had proved to be.

What was more she had left without even paying for her keep!

'At least this patient looks as if he is wealthy,' Rowena thought.

But she knew that if they were to extract any money from him it would be her task to do so. It would never enter her father's head to ask for his fees to be paid.

The four men carried the gentleman into the bed-room and laid him down on the bed.

When his head was on the pillow, Rowena was able to see that he was extremely handsome, despite the fact that there was a large cut on his forehead which was bleeding profusely.

His eyes were closed and she had the idea there might be further injuries to his body to produce such complete unconsciousness.

"Be there anythin' else us can do, Miss Rowena?" Abe asked.

"Yes, there is, Abe," Rowena said briskly. "You had best undress the gentleman and get him into bed. There is no-one else to attend to him except Mrs. Hanson and myself, and the Doctor will be too busy when he returns."

The men looked at the recumbent gentleman a little nervously, as if they were afraid he might awake and curse them for such familiarity.

"Handle him gently," Rowena insisted, "I will fetch one of my father's night-shirts for him."

She went from the room as she spoke, thinking the men might as well make themselves useful and save her father the task when he returned.

She knew from long experience that it was very difficult to undress a large man, especially one who was unconscious.

She was also sure that the gentleman's elegant and expensive clothes would fit far too tightly for them to be removed easily.

She went next door to her father's bed-room and found his night-shirts neatly folded in a drawer where she had arranged them.

She was about to take one off the top of the pile, but then she delved further into the drawer and drew out one which she considered to be his best.

It was of silk and had been made by her mother some years ago as a special present.

"I have always wished that your father could afford silk night-shirts," she said to Rowena with a smile as she sewed the seams with exquisitely small stitches.

"I should have thought it was more important for you, Mama, to have lovely clothes, not Papa," Rowena had replied.

Her mother smiled.

"I do not think your father would notice whether I was dressed in silk or sacking! He loves me just as I am, but I have always wanted the best for him."

That was true, Rowena knew, but it was impossible for either of them to have the best when they had four children. It was never a question of silk night-shirts for her father, but boots for Mark, stockings for Hermione, and gowns for Lotty.

Rowena could never remember a time when it had not been a struggle to feed and clothe themselves.

Sometimes she resented the fact that her father, dedicated to his profession, was completely happy as long as he was helping other people and had no idea of the sacrifices it entailed for his family.

"Do you realise," she had said only a week ago, "that Farmer Bostock has not paid you for the operation you did on his hand over a year ago?"

"Times have been hard for the Bostocks recently," her father replied. "He will pay me when he can afford it."

"How can we afford to live if no-one pays their debts?" Rowena demanded angrily.

But her protests fell on deaf ears and she knew that even if Farmer Bostock or any of her father's other patients paid up, the money as likely as not would go to provide milk for some sick child, or medicines for an invalid who could not afford them for himself.

"I shall see that this patient pays, if it is the last thing I do," Rowena promised herself as she took the night-shirt next door and knocked at the door.

She was not shy or squeamish about seeing a man being undressed and had in fact often helped her father when there had been a patient in the house and no-one else to attend to him.

But she knew that Abe and the other villagers would be extremely shocked at the thought of her looking at the gentleman until he was between the sheets.

So she merely handed the night-shirt through the door and went downstairs to get some hot water, towels and bandages.

"They have brought a gentleman here who has been involved in an accident, Mrs. Hanson," she told the old cook who was bending over the ancient, temperamental stove in the kitchen.

"What's that, Miss Rowena?" Mrs. Hanson asked.

Anything that was said to the old woman had to be repeated twice, which was because she did not trouble to listen the first time.

"A patient, is it?" Mrs. Hanson asked when Rowena had repeated her words.

There was resentment in the Cook's old eyes because she knew it meant extra work, and Rowena, anxious to keep the peace, said soothingly:

"He looks rich so he will not stay long. When Papa has patched him up there will doubtless be a carriage to collect him, so we need not worry ourselves."

"As if there's not enough in this house to do as it is!" Mrs. Hanson grumbled.

"I do not think our visitor will be wanting anything to eat at the moment," Rowena replied.

She took a china basin from the cupboard and filled a jug with hot water from the kettle on the stove. Then carrying them from the kitchen she went to a cupboard where she kept the bandages her father so often required and a pile of fresh linen towels.

She was just about to climb the stairs again when the four men came trooping down.

"Us has put him into bed, Miss Rowena," Abe said. "Never stirred an eye-lid, he didn't! Reckon th' Doctor'll find him half-dead when he gets here."

He imparted this information with relish, and Rowena knew there was nothing they enjoyed more than the drama of death.

"Thank you all very much," she said, "but I have a feeling that our new patient will survive, especially in my father's magic hands."

"That's right enough, Miss Rowena," Abe said. "The Doctor's got a way wi' him that's nothing short o' miraculous! That's what me wife said when he dragged her back from th' very grave itself!"

"A lot of people have said the same thing," Rowena smiled.

The man opened the front door.

"If there be anything else ye wants, Miss Rowena, ye has only t' ask. We be goin' back now to clear up th' mess at th' cross-roads. Oi hopes we don't have t' bring ye no-one else."

"There is no room for anyone else," Rowena said sharply. "Make that clear to my father when you see him and tell him to come back as soon as possible."

"We'll tell th' Doctor, Miss."

The men touched their forelocks respectfully, the door closed behind them, and Rowena started up the stairs.

She entered the bed-room to find the gentleman laid back against the pillows, his clothes placed over a chair by the fireplace.

Rowena set down the basin by the bed-side and poured some of the water from the jug into it. Then she bent over the bed to inspect the cut on the gentleman's forehead.

The blood from it had run over his face and gently she wiped it away with the warm water and saw that the wound, although it looked unpleasant, was not very deep.

'He must have other injuries,' she thought as she wiped his face with a soft towel.

Now he was cleaned up he looked even more handsome then she had thought at first.

He had straight, aristocratic features, a square chin, a firm, almost hard mouth which made her think he might be a difficult man to cross.

She guessed that he was over thirty, and his dark hair was cut in the wind-swept manner which had been made fashionable by the Prince Regent.

'He is obviously someone very important,' she told herself and saw that he had long, thin fingers and on one of them a signet-ring with an elaborate monogram.

She felt there was nothing more she could do except wait for her father's return and automatically she picked up the clothes which lay over the chair.

She noticed the quality of the grey whipcord riding-coat and as she lifted it she saw there was a wallet in the inside breast-pocket.

She took it out to lay it on the dressing-table and realised that it was filled with notes.

She resisted the impulse to open it.

When she lifted the pale champagne-coloured pantaloons she heard the clink of a purse in one of the pockets and taking it out she set it down beside the wallet.

'At least he has money,' she thought with satisfaction, 'and he shall not leave without paying Papa.'

The injured man's polished Hessian boots were dusty, doubtless from the roadway into which he must have been thrown during the collision.

Rowena wondered what had happened to the horses. She could not bear to think that they might have been hurt.

She remembered the last time there had been an accident on the roadway when two horses being driven at an outrageous speed had broken their legs and had had to be destroyed.

She wondered if the gentleman's driving had been at fault.

But she felt certain that he would be an expert with the reins and that the accident had been entirely due to the Stagecoach.

Had Abe not said the driver was drunk?

There were far too many coaches on the road these days driven by drunken, incompetent drivers, many of whom should not have been in control of horses in the first place.

At the same time Rowena had the feeling, perhaps unfairly, that the gentleman had been driving fast.

He did not look the sort of man who would linger on the road; he would be impatient to reach his destination and perhaps that would account for his present position.

She looked around the room to see if there was anything else she could do, but at that moment she heard the front door open, and ran to the top of the stairs to see that her father was already in the hall.

"Papa!" she exclaimed.

"There you are, Rowena! Abe told me they had put the patient to bed."

"He is ready and waiting for you, Papa. Was it a very bad accident?"

"Rather a mess," Dr. Winsford replied as he came up the stairs.

"What happened?"

"The driver of the Stage-coach took the corner on the wrong side of the road. It was entirely his fault and only by superb driving did the man in charge of the Phaeton save his horses from a head-on collision."

"I thought it would be the Stage-coach driver's fault."

"God looks after drunkards and fools, so he escaped without a scratch," the Doctor said. "But this poor devil had his Phaeton overturned and I rather suspect that the wheel went over him."

"Is he really bad, Papa?"

"I cannot know until I have examined him," the Doctor replied. "Will you bring me some hot water?"

"It is there in the bed-room already," Rowena answered,

"and I have washed the blood from his face. His forehead does not look too bad."

"It is his internal injuries I am concerned about," Dr. Winsford replied. "Have you left some bandages?"

"Yes, Papa, they are already there."

Dr. Winsford walked into the bed-room.

He looked towards the bed and said:

"You have undressed him – good girl! It saves time and there are a dozen scratches, bruises and bleeding noses for me to attend to at the Plough and Sickle!"

Her father walked across the bed-room as he spoke to wash his hands in the basin on the wash-hand-stand.

"Is there anything else you want, Papa?" Rowena asked.

"No, I think I have everything," her father replied vaguely.

He was looking at the patient on the bed as he dried his hands and Rowena knew he was concentrating on the injured man which prevented him from thinking of anything else.

"I will go and make you a cup of tea, Papa," she said. "Call if you want me."

She ran down the stairs glad to have something to do for her father.

She knew only too well how accidents such as this upset him: it was part of what the villagers thought of as his miraculous powers that he was actually sensitive and hated to see people suffering pain of any sort.

Rowena could visualise the screaming women and children from the Stage-coach, the horses plunging and neighing with fear, the shouts of the men and the fallen bodies of those who had been hurt mixed up with the luggage thrown off the Stage-coach, the coops of hens and more likely than not a goat or a sheep sewn up into a sack.

Most of all her father, like herself, would wince from the injuries inflicted on the horses.

She was quite certain that the gentleman who had been hurt would be driving superlative horse-flesh and she only hoped that they had not been pierced by a broken shaft or blinded as recently a horse had been in a collision which had occurred in a neighbouring village.

"Is th' Doctor home?" Mrs. Hanson asked as Rowena entered the kitchen.

"Yes, he is upstairs with the patient."

"I were to tell him, Miss Rowena, that Mistress Carstairs would appreciate if he'd call in to see her this eve."

"He will not have time for that," Rowena replied firmly. "You know as well as I do, Mrs. Hanson, that all Mrs. Carstairs requires is some-one to listen to her grumbles about her son. There is nothing wrong with her and she just wastes Papa's time, only he is far too kind to say so."

"I'm only a-passing on the message as I receives it from the kitchen-door," Mrs. Hanson replied.

"Yes, I know," Rowena answered, "but I think we will just forget it in the excitement over the accident."

Mrs. Carstairs was only one of many who imposed upon her father's good nature, she thought.

He was not only the Physician for the village, he was the confidant, the Father Confessor, and at times she teased him by saying he was almost a fortune-teller as well!

"There is nothing they do not expect of you," she would say. "It is time that lazy Vicar took some of these people off your hands."

"They trust me," Dr. Winsford had replied gently. "I must not fail them, Rowena."

As she went upstairs carrying her father's tea on a neatly arranged tray, she thought that now her mother was dead her father immersed himself even more completely in his work than he had done before.

She was sure that it was because when he was working he did not have to think about the wife he had lost, who had left an aching void in his life which no-one, not even his children, could fill.

Rowena knew he was fond of her and relied on her, but no-one however willing, could take her mother's place and as far as her father was concerned, when she had died, the light had gone out of his life.

It had all happened so swiftly and Rowena often thought unnecessarily.

It had been a hard, cold winter and her mother had developed a cough which persisted despite the fact that they tried various home-made remedies.

The house had been cold since they could not afford much coal, and money had been so short that they had not always even had enough to eat.

Looking back when it was too late, Rowena was certain that her mother deprived herself so that her husband and children could have the lion's share of everything there was.

Her cough had grown worse until suddenly they found she had developed pneumonia, and without the strength to resist it she had died suddenly to leave her family shattered by the blow.

"If everybody had paid you what they owed," Rowena said bitterly after the funeral, "I am sure Mama would be alive to-day."

Her father had not answered, and she would not worry him any further.

But Rowena decided with a determination which made her thrust out her small chin that never again would she allow patients who could afford it to get away without paying their bills.

The local notabilities, and there were not many of them, were astonished to receive letters written by Rowena in her elegant hand, setting out how many attendances her father had made on them and asking that he should be paid as soon as possible.

When this failed she did not hesitate to arrive in person.

"I must say, Miss Winsford," the butcher's wife said acidly, "your father has never harassed us like this in the past."

"With the result, Mrs. Pitt, that we often go hungry," Rowena replied.

The Butcher's wife was astonished.

"Do you really mean that, Miss Winsford?"

"I am sure your husband will tell you, Mrs. Pitt, that we have not ordered any meat for the last week," Rowena replied, "and that is simply because we have not the money with which to pay for it."

The butcher's wife had paid, as had several other well-to-do residents of Little Powick, but the majority of her father's patients had not a penny to bless themselves with.

Although Dr. Winsford actually spent more time on them than on the well-to-do, Rowena treated them as objects of charity.

Sometimes however, she could not help thinking that charity should begin at home, especially when she contemplated her extremely scanty wardrobe, and the fact that she had to spend every moment of her spare time making clothes for her sisters and brother.

She opened the door of the bed-room and carried in her father's tray of tea.

He had his shirt-sleeves rolled up and was just putting the sheets and blankets back over his patient.

"I have brought you some tea, Papa."

"Thank you," Dr. Winsford replied vaguely.

"He is bad?" Rowena asked.

"Bad enough," the Doctor replied. "I fancy there are two or three ribs cracked and his stomach is bruised, but it is hard to tell what may have been damaged inside."

"Have you any idea who he is?"

"Yes. His groom told me. He is the Marquis of Swayne."

"The Marquis of Swayne?" Rowena repeated with wide eyes. "Surely he lives at Swayneling Park, that huge house near Hatfield?"

"That is correct," Dr. Winsford answered.

"What are you going to do about him?" Rowena enquired.

"His groom, who was not injured, is driving home to tell them what has happened. I expect he will have a secretary or someone who will get in touch with us, although I am sure he should not be moved until he has been examined by a Specialist."

"A Specialist?" Rowena exclaimed. "Where do you think we can find one around here?"

"Doubtless they will send to London," Dr. Winsford replied. "I imagine it will not be an extravagance where the Marquis is concerned."

He smiled at his daughter as he spoke and the smile illuminated his thin face.

He had been an exceedingly handsome man and those who had known him in the past could understand why his children were all so outstandingly good-looking.

"Do not look so worried, my dear," Dr. Winsford went on. "I am quite certain that the noble Marquis will not trouble us for long, and quite frankly the sooner he is in expert hands the better!"

"I doubt if it will be better for him, Papa," Rowena answered. "You know as well as I do that you have what the old women call 'healing fingers', and I doubt if any Specialist would be able to do more for him than you can."

"I wish that were true," Dr. Winsford replied, "but I am well aware of my own limitations."

. . . . . .

The Marquis lay with closed eyes and wondered where he was.

He felt very weak and tired, but the fog which had seemed to fill his head and prevent him from thinking had cleared, and he was aware now that there was someone in the room.

It was a person who walked very quietly and he thought he had been aware of her presence for some time, but it had been impossible to concentrate.

As he thought about it, he felt an arm slipped under the back of his head, and he was lifted very gently, to feel the edge of a cup against his lips.

"Try to drink a little," a soft voice said.

Almost automatically he responded to the voice and felt that this was not the first time he had obeyed it.

What he swallowed tasted sweet and delicious, and because he realised he was thirsty and his throat hurt he drank a little more.

"That is very good," the voice said approvingly. "Now go to sleep again and I will bring you some beef-tea a little later on."

"Why cannot I have some beef-tea?" someone asked.

The Marquis was aware that it was the high-pitched voice of a child.

"Lotty, how often have I told you, you are not to come into this room?" the first voice asked.

"But I like to look at him," Lotty replied defiantly, "Hermione says he looks like a fallen Gladiator. I think she is in love with him!"

"You are not to talk such nonsense! Go downstairs at once and neither you nor Hermione are to come in here again. Is that understood?"

"I think you are very selfish, Rowena, to keep him all to yourself," Lotty objected. "We want to look at him too."

"Go downstairs at once!"

There was a note of authority in Rowena's voice which apparently had its effect, because the Marquis heard the patter of feet down the stairs and Rowena, whoever she might be, crossed the room to close the door.

Very slowly, half-afraid that the mere action of raising his eye-lids might start up again the pain in his head which the Marquis recalled as being intolerable, he opened his eyes.

He saw, as he had expected, that he was in a strange room and that he was lying in a strange bed.

Standing by the wash-hand-stand, washing the cup out of which he had recently drunk, was the slim figure of a woman.

She had her back to him, and remembering the softness of her voice and the gentleness with which she had raised him the Marquis found himself waiting for her to turn so that he could see her face.

She dried the cup and set it down on the saucer with an infinitesimal amount of noise, then she placed the cloth on a towel-rail and turned towards him.

He had somehow expected her to resemble her voice, but was not prepared for what he saw and thought for one second she must be an hallucination due to concussion.

Nearing his bed was a girl, she was obviously little more, who was lovelier than anyone he had seen for a long time.

She was concentrating on her thoughts, and her large eyes which seemed almost to fill her thin face were not really looking at him until she reached his side.

Then as her hands went out to tidy the sheet which had been disarrayed while he drank, she saw that he was looking at her and stood still.

"You are awake?" she questioned.

She did not wait for his reply but said quickly:

"Do not try to talk. You have been unconscious for a long time, but now I think you can hear me. There is no reason to be worried or afraid. You are in good hands."

Despite her instructions the Marquis managed to speak although his voice sounded strange and hoarse.

"Where – am I?"

"You are at Little Powick where you had an accident."

Rowena paused as if to let this sink in. Then she said:

"No-one was hurt except you, and I am sure you will want to know that your horses, although frightened, were not hurt or injured in any way."

"I am – glad to hear that, but – who are – you?"

"I am the doctor's daughter, Rowena Winsford."

"Doctor – Winsford?" the Marquis repeated as if he was trying to recollect the name.

He saw the smile that illuminated Rowena's face.

"You will not have heard of us," she said, "but your Specialist, Sir George Seymour, came from London to see you. He said that there was nothing wrong with you that

23

would not mend itself, but he utterly refused to have you moved."

As Rowena spoke she saw the Marquis's eyes close as if he was weary.

"Go to sleep," she said softly. "There is nothing to trouble you. You will be well enough to go home in a few days."

* * * * *

The Marquis sat up in bed with difficulty and regarded the tray that had been set down in front of him.

"I do not like pigeon!" he said positively.

"I am afraid there is nothing else," Rowena replied. "Chickens are expensive and you had beef yesterday."

"If he does not like pigeon," came a voice from the door, "can he have my Shepherd's Pie? I love pigeon – so does Hermione!"

The Marquis turned his head to see Lotty, whom he knew well by now, looking at him pleadingly from the door.

She was with her large eyes and fair hair a replica of her older sister. But while Rowena's face was thin to match the extreme slenderness of her body, Lotty was round and plump and looked, the Marquis thought, rather like one of the carvings of a small angel in a Bavarian Church.

He was not however to be diverted from his train of thought.

"Why is chicken too expensive?" he asked.

"Because we have not the money with which to buy it, My Lord," Rowena replied.

"Are you telling me that I am not paying for my keep?" he enquired.

"You have not been in a fit state until now for me to ask you for money," Rowena replied.

"Then why did you not ask my secretary? He is here often enough."

"I never thought of it," Rowena said frankly.

"Then why the devil did he not offer it?" the Marquis questioned irritably.

"He brought you some fruit which we could not have afforded to buy, and the wine which Papa does not really approve of your drinking until your head is better."

"I suppose it never crossed his mind that you could not afford to buy every luxury," the Marquis said almost as if he spoke to himself. "Anyway, I have some money with me."

"It is here, My Lord, in the drawer of the dressing-table."

"Then bring it to me."

"Your food is getting cold," she answered, "and I suggest you eat first."

The Marquis looked towards Lotty.

"I think I would rather have the Shepherd's Pie."

"I will fetch it for you – I will fetch it at once!" Lotty cried.

"No – wait!" Rowena called, but it was too late.

Already her small sister was half-way down the stairs.

"If you interfere with my housekeeping arrangements," she said to the Marquis, "I shall send you home immediately, whatever the doctors say!"

"You have bullied me long enough," the Marquis answered, "I shall stay here just as long as it suits me, and you know as well as I do that your father will not turn me out!"

"My father has plenty of patients besides you!"

"But not such important ones!" he said with a smile.

"I consider that a very conceited remark," Rowena replied. "Where suffering is concerned, to Papa all men are equal."

"But, as you are aware, some can afford to pay," the Marquis answered.

There was no answer to this and Rowena pressed her lips together to prevent herself from replying in what she felt would be an undignified manner.

She had already found that since the Marquis was better he could be extremely obstinate, and often challenged her in a manner which she found annoying because she considered it undermined her authority.

Lotty, she told herself now as she heard her younger sister coming up the stairs, would not have dared a week ago to demand pigeon when she was supposed to be eating Shepherd's Pie.

Now she came into the room carrying it on a plate and handed it to the Marquis.

"Thank you," he said. "That looks very appetising."

"May I have your pigeon?" Lotty asked almost breathlessly.

"With pleasure!" the Marquis replied.

She took the plate from his tray.

"Half for me and half for Mark," she said. "Hermione has already eaten her Shepherd's Pie so she will not want any."

The Marquis picked up his fork while Lotty went downstairs again carrying the pigeon carefully in both hands.

"I would like to point out," Rowena said, "that we are trying to build up Your Lordship's strength. There is far more nourishment in a pigeon than there is in a Shepherd's Pie which consists mostly of potato."

"I presume," the Marquis said, "that it had been made from what was left of the meat that you gave me yesterday?"

"I am astonished you should know what ingredients constitute a Shepherd's Pie," Rowena replied. "I am quite certain you have never been obliged to eat one before."

"I find it surprisingly appetising," the Marquis replied, "and now, as I am no longer hungry, let us get back to the subject of money."

"Not until you have eaten your junket," Rowena said.

She brought the dish and a plate from the top of the chest-of-drawers as she spoke.

"It is good for you," she said as she set it down in front of him, "and there are some fresh raspberries from the garden to go with it."

"You are are quite certain Lotty does not want those?"

"Lotty is greedy and you are not to encourage her."

The Marquis took a spoonful of junket which he could not

26

remember eating since he was a boy, and found it very palatable.

"Tell me about yourself," he asked.

"There is nothing to tell," Rowena answered. "You have seen us all by now and you must be aware that we are an ordinary doctor's family living quietly in a small village with no excitement except what is provided by bad driving on the main road."

The Marquis's eyes flashed for a moment as if he suspected she was deliberately trying to needle him. Then he said:

"You certainly do not look like an ordinary doctor's family."

Rowena smiled.

"I think Hermione is going to be a beauty. Already the choir-boys find it almost impossible to sing when she is in Church!"

"I agree with you," the Marquis said, "and you, if you came to London, would certainly stop the traffic in Piccadilly!"

Rowena looked at him as if she thought he was making fun of her. Then seeing the expression in his eyes she said quickly:

"You must not try to turn our heads, My Lord, and please do not flatter Hermione. She is romantic enough to think she is in love with you, and when you have left I shall have a difficult time making her settle down again to her lessons and good works."

"Is that the only future you envisage for the poor girl?"

"What else is there?" Rowena asked almost defiantly.

She found that ever since the Marquis had arrived in their home he had proved a very disturbing influence.

It was impossible for her not to be positively aware of him, both by day and by night, not only because she waited on him but also because he had brought into their house something she had never known before.

It was like a blustery wind blowing through the small

rooms, or finding the blinding sun in one's face when one least expected it.

Even while he was unconscious he had been, she thought, distinctly masculine.

Now he was awake she could talk to him, argue with him, and there was something about him which challenged her.

She thought that he infuriated her with his calm assumption that he was of such extreme importance that the whole world must be prepared to bow and do his bidding.

She also found it impossible not to feel that he was condescending in staying with them when he had huge, important houses in which he would be far more comfortable.

His secretary called to see him driving in a Curricle drawn by horses so fine that it made Rowena feel breathless even to look at them.

His valet who came over every day to attend to him increased Rowena's knowledge of the Marquis's vast possessions and the distinguished place he held in Society, which at the same time made her feel more and more insignificant.

The Marquis drank the glass of claret which stood on the tray.

"I would like some more wine," he said.

'One glass is all you are allowed," Rowena answered.

"Nonsense!" he said. "I am thirsty and I require another glass. Pour it out for me."

Rowena almost obeyed him, then changed her mind.

"You must ask my father," she said. "As far as I am concerned I carry out the doctor's orders – not yours."

He smiled in a manner which made her feel uncertain of herself.

"You are punishing me," he said, "because I allowed Lotty to have my pigeon. Stop being a dictatorial Amazon and give me another glass of claret."

"And if I refuse?"

"Then I shall get out of bed and get it myself!"

"You would not dare!"

"Are you certain about that?" he enquired.

Their eyes met and she had the feeling that it was a battle of wills. Having an uncomfortable conviction that he would do what he said, she capitulated.

"Very well," she said. "Have it your own way, and if you have a splitting headache to-night do not blame me."

"Surely you know that a patient should always be humoured?" the Marquis asked.

He was watching with satisfaction as she filled his glass from the cut-glass decanter which his valet had brought with the wine from Swayneling Park.

Rowena did not answer and the Marquis said:

"Why the silence? I am used to your trying to cap every remark I make, so I feel quite worried when you do not reply."

"I am keeping my thoughts to myself because I do not think you are well enough to hear them," Rowena answered.

The Marquis smiled.

"That is more like it! Now bring me my wallet."

"I have kept an account of what I consider you owe my father," Rowena said. "Do you wish to see it?"

"Naturally!"

She opened a drawer, took it out and brought it to the bed-side.

He read it slowly, then he said:

"My dear girl, this is ridiculous! Do you really imagine that I value your father's services at less than half what I pay my vet for looking after my horses?"

"Papa will be quite content to receive that amount."

"I will pay your father later what I consider he is worth," the Marquis said. "Again what you charge for my board and lodging is quite ridiculous!"

"It is more than I have ever asked of anyone else," Rowena replied, then she smiled. "In most cases that was too much."

The Marquis drew some notes from his wallet.

"Here is £20," he said. "And let me make this quite clear.

This is for the housekeeping. My debt to your father I will settle with him personally."

Rowena took a step backwards almost as if he had struck her.

"D . do you .. really think I would accept such a .. large sum for you?" she asked.

"You have no alternative," he replied, "and if you are going to be difficult about it I shall merely send my secretary to put a deposit in your name with the local tradesmen."

"You will do no such thing!" Rowena cried angrily, "and let me make it quite clear, we are not asking for charity, My Lord."

"I am asking for luxuries," the Marquis replied. "You said I needed to build up my strength. Very well, I require legs of lamb, sirloins of beef, plump chickens and a number of other things, many of which, now I think of it, can be procured from my own home."

"We will not accept them!" Rowena cried.

"You disappoint me," the Marquis said. "I had begun to think that you could be quite a good business woman. Instead I see you are merely a humbug, feeding the rich at the expense of the poor for some obscure and quite unjustified pride, which in reality is something you simply cannot afford."

"How dare you speak to me like that!"

But Rowena knew as she spoke that while she might try to oppose him they needed all the things the Marquis was prepared to offer them.

Because it would be of benefit to the children she would in the end capitulate and he would have his own way.

CHAPTER TWO

"Can I come in?" a voice whispered from the doorway.

The Marquis turned his head a little to see Hermione peeping in at him.

"Yes, come in," he replied.

"Rowena will be annoyed if she finds me here, but I wanted to show you my new gown."

The Marquis had suffered a relapse a few days ago and Sir George had come from London again to prescribe complete quiet.

"It is only a fever," he told Dr. Winsford, "and it is what might be expected. I am quite certain that there is nothing wrong with him which rest and quiet cannot cure."

The Marquis however felt extremely ill. His headache had returned and he was glad when the medications he took made him sleep deeply, unconscious of everything including his pain.

When he was awake he was aware that Rowena had become the soft, gentle person she had been when he first came to consciousness after his accident.

He found himself listening for the sweetness of her voice and waiting for the softness of her arm when she lifted his head so that he could drink.

But now he was better and he smiled at Hermione as she advanced towards the bed, obviously very conscious of the pretty new muslin gown she wore.

It was, the Marquis saw with an experienced eye, of a cheap material, but the periwinkle blue matched the vivid blue of her eyes and was a perfect frame for the purity of her skin.

He thought, not for the first time, that Hermione would be sensational in a year or so if she were properly gowned and presented to the Social World.

But he had learnt by this time that there was no possibility of this ever taking place.

He could not help feeling that it was rather sad that these beautiful girls should be incarcerated in the small village of Little Powick where nobody would ever see them.

While Rowena and Lotty were outstandingly lovely in a classical manner, Hermione's beauty hit one almost with the force of a sledge-hammer.

Rowena's fair hair was so pale that it almost had silver lights in it, but Hermione's was positively and vividly gold.

Rowena and Lotty's eyes were the soft blue of a thrush's egg, while Hermione's were the deep blue of gentians so vivid that one felt almost blinded by them.

'How could an ordinary country doctor have produced such exquisite creatures,' the Marquis wondered as he had done a dozen times before.

"Do you like it?" Hermione asked anxiously.

She was standing by his bed-side in her new gown and now she pirouetted round so that he could see her from every angle.

"You look very attractive," the Marquis said, "but I expect you are aware of that already."

"I wanted you to think I look pretty," Hermione said with a little glance at him from under her eye-lashes which would undoubtedly, the Marquis thought with amusement, have made a younger man's heart stop beating.

"Did you make it yourself?" he enquired.

"I did a great deal of it," Hermione replied proudly. "Rowena cut it out for me, but I sewed all the seams and arranged the frills around the neck and sleeves."

She gave a little sigh.

"I wish someone would ask me to a party. There are never any parties in Little Powick."

"What about the County? Surely there are people outside the village?" the Marquis asked.

Hermione smiled at him.

"You know as well as I do," she said, "that the County families are very puffed up with their own importance. If they give a Ball or a Reception, the children of doctors do not qualify."

The Marquis did not reply because he knew this was true.

"When the old Squire was alive," Hermione went on, "Papa and Mama were asked to dinner once a year. Papa used to hate going, but Mama would laugh and say his evening clothes enjoyed the outing."

The Marquis remembered that this was how his father had treated their local doctor. If he had had any children the Marquis could not remember them, but he was quite certain they would not have resembled in any way the Winsfords.

"Mama used to say that everyone should have a hobby," Hermione announced, obviously following the train of her own thoughts.

"And what is yours?" the Marquis enquired.

"Drawing pictures of beautiful gowns!" Hermione replied. "What I would like to do if I had the chance, is to design gowns that could be made up by an expensive dressmaker."

"I should have thought that was a rather good idea," the Marquis said.

"I need lessons," Hermione said with a sigh, "it is very difficult to know if what you do is right or wrong without a teacher."

"Surely you are being educated?" the Marquis enquired.

"Of course we are!" Hermione replied. "Mama was very insistent on that, but Papa can only afford to pay for subjects that matter, like history, geography, arithmetic, which I hate, and English Literature."

"Is that an essential subject?"

"Rowena thinks it is. She said we would be very ignorant if we did not read and we must try to develop a critical faculty."

"And you think you are doing that?" the Marquis enquired with a smile.

"I would much rather be drawing," Hermione replied, "but when I suggested it to Rowena she said no."

"Rowena also said you were not to come into this bedroom!" a voice said from the doorway.

Hermione started round guiltily.

"She came to show me her new gown," the Marquis explained. "I have been admiring your joint handiwork."

"You have to keep very quiet," Rowena said, "and as you well know I have told the children to keep out of this room."

"That was yesterday," the Marquis said. "To-day I feel much better, and I am sure it is bad for me to brood alone."

Rowena brought him a glass of home-made lemonade.

He took a few sips of it and handed it back to her.

"I would like a glass of champagne this evening. Will you tell Johnson?"

Rowena looked doubtful.

"I shall have to ask Papa first."

"It is a waste of time," the Marquis retorted. "You know as well as I do that he will agree to anything which makes me feel better."

"Very well, I will tell your valet when he returns," Rowena said a little stiffly.

Hermione looked at the Marquis with a light in her eyes.

"Has Johnson gone to Swayneling Park?" she asked. "If so, perhaps he will bring back some more of those luscious big peaches."

"Hermione!" Rowena exclaimed.

"I shall be very annoyed if he does not bring back fruit and vegetables and anything else you require," the Marquis said.

"You are very kind," Rowena interposed, "but we must not impose on you."

"I need them for my own consumption," the Marquis said, "and I hope to-night I shall be allowed a proper dinner. I am very tired of the slops you have been feeding me for the last few days!"

"You know you were allowed nothing else while you had a fever," she replied.

"I am not really complaining," he answered, "but actually I feel quite hungry."

"You are better – much better!" Hermione said in an excited voice. "That means we can come in and talk to you. It has been awfully boring having to tip-toe past your room when there were so many things we wanted to ask you."

"What did you want to ask?" the Marquis enquired.

"That is quite enough, Hermione!" Rowena interposed. "Run along now. His Lordship has talked long enough."

She saw the disappointment on her sister's face and added:

"Perhaps if he is not too tired you can come back later and say good-night to him."

"I want to stay and talk to him now," Hermione insisted.

"We were talking about hobbies," the Marquis said to Rowena. "Your sister informs me that she wishes to be a dress-designer."

"She is just as likely to jump over the moon," Rowena said crossly.

"Mama said everybody should have a hobby," Hermione repeated defiantly. "What is yours, My Lord?"

"As a matter of fact I have a hobby which I enjoy very much," the Marquis replied. "I wonder if you can guess what it is?"

"Is it something to do with horses?"

"No."

He looked at Rowena.

"I am sure whatever it is," she remarked, "it is very expensive and undoubtedly personal."

"It is not particularly expensive," the Marquis replied, "but it is certainly personal and I find it absorbing."

"What is it?" Hermione asked. "Do tell us."

"Genealogy," he replied.

Hermione looked blank and the Marquis turned to Rowena as if challenging her to explain.

"I think," she said slowly, "that it has to do with one's ancestors."

"That is correct," the Marquis said. "It is the history of the origins of one's family."

"Does it mean that you are making your family tree?" Hermione asked. "There is a picture of one in one of the history books I am reading. I think it is of King Charlemagne."

"A very good example," the Marquis replied, "and mine, as a matter of fact goes back before William the Conqueror and includes no less than four Kings."

"I call that a very exciting hobby," Hermione said admiringly.

Rowena said nothing and the Marquis looking at her profile said:

"I feel quite sure that in your practical mind, Rowena, you consider my preoccupation a waste of time."

"I imagine, My Lord, you have a lot of time to waste," Rowena replied, "but here in this house we are more concerned with the living than the dead."

"That is exactly what I expected you to say," he remarked, and she felt annoyed that she had not thought of something more original.

She did not know why, but the moment the Marquis was better again they seemed to fence with each other, engaging in a duel of words which was at times stimulating, at others slightly embarrassing.

There was something about the Marquis which made her want to fight him.

It was, she told herself, not at all the attitude she should take towards a patient, and yet when he was not in pain, asleep or unconscious she found his air of superiority extremely irritating.

He was so sure of himself; he looked so distinguished and authoritative; and she felt somewhat resentfully he had become the centre of attention for the whole family.

When they were all together, Hermione, Mark and Lotty

could talk of nothing but the Marquis, and she was well aware that Hermione not only thought of him but dreamt about him at night.

Mark had lessons most of the day, but no sooner had he returned to the house than he had a hundred questions to ask about their important patient.

If any of the Marquis's horses were in the stable he would fling down his lesson-books and rush out to see them.

Once the Marquis had discovered how poor they were, the food which was brought to the house was a delight they had never known before.

On his instructions not only chickens, young turkeys and pigeons arrived daily from Swayneling Park, but also lamb and mutton from his own sheep, and beef from his own oxen.

Lotty and Mark could not get over the enormous size of the peaches from the greenhouses or the baskets of grapes, nectarines, greengages and plums.

These arrived in such profusion that Rowena's store cupboard in the kitchen which was usually empty was now filled with jams, chutneys and preserves which she and Mrs. Hanson made before a lot of the fruit could go bad.

Mrs. Hanson recovered very quickly from her resentment at having another mouth to feed when a kitchen-maid from Swayneling Park came over to help her and not only prepared the vegetables but was also ready to scrub the floor of the kitchen.

It was only Rowena who felt resentful that the Marquis seemed to have taken over the house.

His valet and the kitchen-maid arrived in the morning and left in the evening bringing with them in a Landau the great hampers of food.

Mr. Ashburn, the Marquis's secretary, also called every day and never left without asking Rowena if there was anything she wanted for his Lordship's comfort.

As he too exuded an aura of superiority and gave the impression that he did not consider the surroundings suitable for his master, Rowena with difficulty prevented herself from replying that the one thing she really wanted was that the Marquis should remove to his own home as soon as possible.

But this she knew neither her father nor the Specialist would permit.

She could not help feeling however that the Marquis's disruptive influence would make it very hard to return to normal once he had gone.

'He is spoiling the children for the life they will have to lead in the future,' she thought to herself.

Now, because she wished to prick the balloon of his self-importance, she said:

"I should have thought Your Lordship would have found something more active to do than delving into dusty manuscripts to see which of your antecedents produced an all-important son to carry on the name."

"I am not alone in my hobby," the Marquis replied. "Julius Caesar for instance, boasted of his descent from Aeneas, who doubtless you will remember was not only a Trojan hero but also the son of Aphrodite."

"Do you really expect me to believe that Aphrodite ever existed?" Rowena enquired.

"I think perhaps you and Hermione are living proof of that," the Marquis replied with a twist of his lips which was undoubtedly mocking.

"I want to know about Genealogy – tell me about it," Hermione begged. "If you find it interesting, it must be."

"Thank you," the Marquis replied.

Rowena thought that because he felt it would annoy her he began to explain to Hermione how Genealogy had started with epic poems like those of Homer and the Nordic Sagas, and had even been significant in Greek history in the 5th century.

"What did they write it on, and can we read what they wrote?" Hermione enquired.

"They used papyrus and later parchment," the Marquis said. "The Priests of Thebes in Egypt had 345 wooden statues, each of which represented an ancestor of a distinct generation."

"That must have been fun," Hermione exclaimed. "I would like to have statues of our family. But there would not be many of them. I suppose you have hundreds."

"Thousands more likely," the Marquis said complacently, "and of course the Romans studied Genealogy to show the distinction between the Patricians and the Plebeians."

"Which we are," Rowena said sharply, "and now it is time, My Lord, for you to rest. Come along, Hermione, you know you should be laying the table."

"I always have to go and do something else just when I am interested," Hermione replied resentfully. "I am sure it is better for my mind to listen to His Lordship than count how many cups and saucers there are on the table."

Nevertheless, because she always obeyed Rowena, she went out of the room giving the Marquis a glance over her shoulder as she said:

"I want to hear a lot more, My Lord, and I would like to see your family tree."

"I will show it to you," the Marquis promised.

Rowena adjusted the blind so that the light sunshine should not disturb the Marquis.

"I am sorry that my hobby does not interest you," he said from the bed.

"It is not that," Rowena corrected.

She turned back from the window and walked towards him.

"Then what is it?" he asked.

"I know you mean to be kind, My Lord," she replied, "and I appreciate all the things you have given us since you have been here."

She paused to choose her words with care as she continued:

"But I do not want you to encourage the children to the point where they will miss you so much when you have left that their home will seem a very dull place."

"I think you are flattering me," the Marquis said.

"I am not doing that," Rowena retorted sharply, "I am only realising very clearly that, while we are not of the least importance in your life, you are becoming very important in ours."

She gave a little sigh before she went on:

"Mark can talk of nothing but your horses, and your groom has let him ride one or two of them. How do you think he is going to feel when there is only old Dobbin to jog about on, when my father is not using him to visit his patients?"

"Surely you think it is good for a boy of Mark's age to be interested in horse-flesh?" the Marquis asked.

"Interested .. yes!" Rowena retorted, "but obsessed .. no! Especially with the kind of horses that he is never likely to see again, let alone ride."

The Marquis did not answer and after a moment she said:

"Hermione, as you know, thinks you are the most attractive and exciting man in the world! With you as her standard of what a man should be, is she ever likely to be content with the very ordinary young men she is likely to meet in a year or two's time?"

"Again you are flattering me," the Marquis said.

"I am not thinking about you," Rowena said. "You will go away, you will return to the life that should never have encroached at any time upon ours."

The Marquis made a restless movement, but he did not interrupt and she continued:

"Doubtless within a few weeks of leaving here you will have forgotten our very existence, and will never so much as give us a passing thought! But I am afraid .. very afraid .. that the impression you leave behind may be inerasable."

Now there was something like a sob in her voice and after a moment the Marquis said:

"There are two members of the family whom so far you have not mentioned – Lotty and yourself."

"Lotty will miss the peaches and all the other good things

with which she has been provided," Rowena answered, "but she does not really constitute a problem like Mark and Hermione."

"And what about yourself?"

"I shall forget you, My Lord, as quickly as possible!"

"And you think that will be easy?"

"I am sure it will be. A meteor does not often pass through the sky and even lightning is said never to strike twice in the same place."

"If I said I would find it hard to forget you, would you believe me?" the Marquis asked.

"I would find it far easier to believe in Aphrodite and all the Greek gods rolled into one."

Rowena walked towards the door before she added:

"It is now time for me to go downstairs and get your tea. I hope Your Lordship will remember what I have said and not encourage either Hermione or Mark."

She left the room before the Marquis could reply, but his eyes were on the door and apparently he was thinking deeply.

*   *   *   *   *

The following afternoon Mr. Ashburn, having made his usual morning call, returned with a box filled with manuscripts.

They were set down beside the Marquis's bed and after the secretary had left Rowena came into the room and glanced at them curiously.

"I thought you might be interested in seeing my family tree, which you were so busy disparaging," the Marquis said. "It is something on which I have worked for a very long time, and I am considering compiling an Almanac of the ancient families of England."

Rowena did not reply and he said:

"As you are so interested I might inform you that the Almanach de Gotha has been published in Germany since 1764 and contains details of all the Sovereign, Princely and Ducal families."

"And you think that one is necessary in England?" Rowena asked.

"Why not?" the Marquis said. "It would certainly be of interest. Do you realise that everything we wish to know about our families has to be culled from the Parish Registers which were not kept before 1538 when Cromwell made it compulsory for all British Priests to keep a Register of births, baptisms and burials."

"I still think, My Lord, that you should concern yourself with the living and see if you can help them," Rowena replied. "Now the war is over, there are thousands of men maimed and crippled, who need assistance and medical treatment. If the newspapers are to be believed, there is a crying need for Orphanages and Homes for Children."

"There are several Orphanages on my Estates," the Marquis replied, "and I believe the Duke of Wellington is very concerned about those wounded in battle. Much as you may disapprove, Rowena, I still enjoy the history of my antecedents."

He opened the box as he spoke and drawing out a large manuscript held it out towards her.

Automatically she took it from him, but when she saw it her expression, which had been one of disdain, changed.

Never had she seen anything so beautiful as the way the manuscript was illustrated with flowers and figures all painted in colours and gold with a precise perfection that was almost that of a miniaturist.

"This represents the part of my family tree," the Marquis explained, "which was compiled in the 14th century by Sir Robert Swayne who was a direct descendant of the Swaynes who invaded these shores with the army of William the Conqueror."

"It is certainly very beautiful," Rowena conceded.

She found it hard to oppose the Marquis when she was looking at anything so lovely.

When he brought manuscript after manuscript from his box she exclaimed over the decorations with minutia and the historiated initials with the same excitement that Hermione might have shown.

There were some illuminated in the French Gothic style which the Marquis said was stimulated by the Patronage of Louis IX.

There were several English scripts of the 14th century with scenes of fantasy and naturalistic foliage like those of the Tickhill Psalter.

There was an exquisite product of Flemish artists of a century later, which showed how the Dukes of Burgundy were related to the Swaynes.

"That is lovely!" Rowena had to exclaim. "But how lucky they have all been preserved!"

"Our family records have been kept very carefully and safely all down the ages," the Marquis replied. "My father was interested in them but not to the extent that I am. I have been collecting these for years."

He smiled as he said:

"We are even mentioned in a history that was written in France by a Father Anselme de St. Marie. It was through that work that I discovered many of the French branches of the Swaynes."

"Are any of them still alive?" Rowena asked.

"A few," he replied.

He showed her several more manuscripts and then replaced them in the carved box in which they had come.

"Now do you understand why I find this hobby absorbing?" he asked.

"To a certain extent," she conceded. "I suppose it makes you even more proud than you would be otherwise."

"Of course!" he answered. "My family now has twenty-five quarterings. My mother was an O'Brien, a family which is directly descended from the Kings of Ireland. Who would not be proud in similar circumstances?"

"I can quite see how hard it will be for you to find a wife for yourself unless you aspire to the Royal Family," Rowena said with a sarcastic note in her voice.

"I had thought of it," the Marquis replied with a twinkle in his eyes, "but the Princesses at Buckingham House are so exceedingly plain that I would find it hard to tolerate their portraits amongst my collection of beautiful ancestresses."

"You could always shut your eyes when you kissed her," Rowena teased, "and recite her family tree beneath your breath."

"That is quite a practical suggestion," the Marquis retorted.

He looked at Rowena as she stood beside the bed.

The sunshine seemed to have been captured by her hair and there was a translucence about her eyes which he had never seen before.

"While we are on the subject of marriage," he remarked, "who do you think you will choose for a husband?"

"As I have such a large selection, you can imagine it is difficult for me to answer that question!"

"Good God! There must be young men somewhere in this part of the world!"

"There is Colonel Dangerfield," Rowena answered, "who tried to kiss me the last time I took him the Parish Magazine. He must be getting on for eighty and is nearly crippled with arthritis, so it was easy to escape his attentions!"

There were two dimples in her cheeks as she went on:

"Then there is a dashing young blade from the Livery stables at Aston Ripley who sometimes comes this way. He offered me a free ride if ever I needed one, but I had the feeling I would have to pay very heavily for the privilege!"

The Marquis made a sound she could not quite interpret, and as she looked at him enquiringly he said:

"Surely you have some relations who would have you to stay and offer you a different sort of life?"

To his surprise Rowena seemed to freeze. Then with the obvious intention of changing the subject she said:

"There is a great deal for me to do downstairs, My Lord. Is there anything you want?"

"Yes, I would like a glass of champagne. Tell Johnson to bring it up."

"Papa said you could drink in moderation and you have already had claret for luncheon to-day."

"Which I intend also to have for dinner," the Marquis replied. "A glass of champagne is a good appetiser."

He saw Rowena's lips tighten and he said:

"Are you really concerned with my health, or are you perhaps thinking I shall retard my recovery and therefore stay with you longer?"

"I am concerned with both," Rowena replied. "You have already had one relapse, My Lord, and I have no wish for you to have another."

"Come here!" the Marquis said in a tone of authority.

A little surprised she obeyed him and when she reached his side he put out his hand.

Because he seemed to compel her to do so she laid her fingers on his.

"I do not wish you to think I am ungrateful," he said. "Sir George has told me in no uncertain terms that I could not have been in better hands than your father's. He also commended the excellent way in which I had been nursed. Thank you, Rowena."

There was a note in his voice which told her he was in fact sincere. Then he raised her hand to his lips and kissed it.

The blood rose in Rowena's cheeks and because she suddenly felt shy and strangely embarrassed her eyes fell before his.

"There is no need to .. thank us, My Lord," she said in a rather breathless little voice, "we have .. simply done our .. duty."

She took her hand away as she spoke.

Then because her heart was beating unaccountably fast and there was a constriction in her throat, she turned and went from the room without looking back.

* * * * *

Dr. Winsford finished his dinner with an absent-minded look in his eyes which told Rowena he had not in fact really appreciated the delicious food which had been brought from Swayneling Park.

There had been trout which had been caught in the lake and chickens – so plump and so succulent that Rowena felt they bore little resemblance to the scraggy cockerels they purchased locally.

The Raspberry Fool had been made with thick Jersey cream from His Lordship's herd, and for dessert there were huge muscat grapes and black cherries.

"Are you worried, Papa?" she asked.

"I have a difficult case where Mrs. Lacey is concerned," Dr. Winsford replied. "As you remember, Rowena, she had twins last week, but she is not recovering as she should, although the twins are thriving."

"They would be!" Rowena replied.

"I am wondering who is going to feed them. Sam Lacey has not done any work for the last year and there are six other children to feed. You would think he would make an effort to find employment."

Her father sighed.

"I grant you he is a ne'er-do-well," he said, "but Mrs. Lacey is an excellent mother. I am just wondering whether, if I should go back there this evening, there is anything I could take her."

"I am sure there is some soup, Papa," Rowena said automatically, "and I dare say there will be some chicken over, although I must leave enough for Mrs. Hanson."

"It will certainly be a help," her father said.

Rowena looked at him sharply.

"You have not been giving Sam Lacey money, have you, Papa?"

Her father immediately looked self-conscious and she knew she had hit the nail on the head.

"Oh, Papa! You promised me over and over again you would not give away money which we cannot afford."

"I should have thought we could afford it at the moment, considering how much the Marquis is paying," the Doctor remarked.

"His Lordship's contribution has paid our back debts and I have a little, a very little, in hand for the future," Rowena said. "You know as well as I do, Papa, we shall soon be back to counting every penny piece and often finding it impossible to buy the food we need."

"I am sorry, Rowena, but I had to help him," Dr. Winsford said quietly.

He rose from the table as he spoke, then bent to kiss his oldest daughter's forehead.

"Do not be too angry with me," he said with a smile, and left the room before she could answer him.

It was always the same, she thought: her father would never face facts! She had been thinking for a long time that they must save money so that Mark could go to school.

He was being taught by a retired teacher in the village and by the Vicar when he could exert himself.

The latter was in fact a very erudite man who had taken First Class Honours at Oxford, but he was extremely idle. The only thing he really enjoyed was hunting in the winter when anyone could be cajoled into supplying him with a horse.

At the same time in his own way he was fond of Dr. Winsford and grateful to him for curing his wife when she had been extremely ill two years ago.

But even with these two teachers Rowena was aware that Mark not only required a far more intensive education than he was receiving, he also needed to mix with boys of his own age.

There were none in the village except the ordinary village lads when they were not working in the fields, most of whom were very rough.

Rowena longed for her brother to be able to go to a Public School such as Harrow or Rugby, where her father had been educated.

'Surely we could manage it somehow,' she thought to herself, but it was difficult to see how.

Although her father agreed in principle that they must save, that did not prevent him from frittering away money on hopeless families like the Laceys.

One thing she told herself was that since the Marquis had been with them she had managed to save almost every shilling that came into the house from other patients.

There were a few conscientious families who tried to pay the Doctor a shilling or so after a confinement, and even as much as three or four shillings after he had set a broken leg, or stitched a damaged head.

This constituted what Rowena thought to herself as 'Mark's Fund'. It was locked away in a box in her bed-room and however hard-pressed they were for housekeeping money she would never encroach on it.

At the same time there was not nearly enough for the fees of any reputable school. Whatever she might have said about the Marquis's effect upon the household, she could not help feeling that his accident might prove to have been a blessing.

But she thought despondently that, even if they could pay for Mark to go to Rugby for one term, they could not carry on with the payments unless wealthy patients like the Marquis dropped out of the skies every other month.

There was no doubt, now that the Marquis was getting better, he would be thinking of leaving.

When she went upstairs to take him a warm drink which she knew would make him sleep well at night, Rowena decided to express something she had been turning over in her mind.

The valet had come as usual to wash and prepare the Marquis for the night and His Lordship was lying back against the pillows wearing one of his own silk night-shirts.

It had the most becoming frills around the neck and they seemed to accentuate the squareness of his chin.

There were frills too at the wrists, and as Rowena moved

towards the bed the last rays of the sun gleamed on the signet-ring on his finger.

Knowing how proud he was of his monogram she smiled a little and thought it was symbolic of his pride in his family and of course in himself.

The Marquis watched her cross the room, thinking he had rarely seen a young woman so graceful or who carried herself as if she wore a crown upon her head.

He had a sudden vision of one of the tiaras that was locked away in the safe at Swayneling Park on her very fair hair.

He knew that the sapphire set would become her, but he decided that the turquoises for which his mother had had such a partiality would be even more striking.

They were surrounded by huge diamonds and on the necklace the great drops of colour would glow vividly against Rowena's white skin.

She came to the bed and sat down on the chair which faced him.

"What is worrying you?" he asked.

She looked surprised that he had noticed before she said:

"Mr. Ashburn was talking to-day as if you would soon be going home."

"Your father says that I may get up for the first time to-morrow. That is a step in the right direction."

Rowena hesitated a moment, then she said:

"I am sure that Sir George Seymour who came down from London twice to see you was very .. expensive."

"I expect so," the Marquis replied carelessly.

"And if you had been .. attended by your usual doctor at home, what would he have .. charged?"

The Marquis looked at her speculatively, then he said:

"Mr. Ashburn can give you that information."

"I would not think of asking such a personal question of your secretary," Rowena said proudly.

"What you are trying to ascertain, is what I intend to pay your father."

"Exactly!" Rowena agreed. "And I wish to ask Your

Lordship whether instead of giving it to Papa you would give the money to me."

"Do you really think that is entirely ethical?"

"If you give it to Papa he will give it away to someone else," Rowena said. "Surely you have realised by now that he treats the villagers not only for their ailments, but also their empty pockets and their empty stomachs."

"And you resent that?"

"Of course I resent it!" Rowena retorted. "It not only deprives my brother and sisters of good food, which is detrimental to their health, but I need the money very urgently for something of great importance."

"A new gown?" the Marquis suggested.

He meant to provoke her and succeeded.

"I am quite aware that you do not have a very high opinion of me," she said witheringly, "but if you think I would embellish myself when my family lack real necessities you are very much mistaken!"

The Marquis laughed and she realised he had been teasing her.

"I am sorry," he said apologetically, "but I find the temptation to make your eyes flash irresistible! I think you must admit that in that skirmish I was the winner."

"I think you are quite detestable!" Rowena snapped.

"Nevertheless, tell me why you need this money so urgently?"

"I want to send Mark to school," Rowena answered simply.

"Mark – Lotty – Hermione!" the Marquis exclaimed. "Do you never think of yourself, Rowena?"

"I am thinking of myself now," she answered. "It breaks my heart to see Mark not only ignorant of so many things he should know, but also without companions of his own age. Do you realise there is not another boy of twelve in the whole of this village who is not a labourer's son?"

She gave a deep sigh before she added quickly:

"That is a stupid question. How should you know? All I

am asking is that you will not give Papa the money you owe, but give it to me. Every penny of it will be spent on Mark."

"You think that will be enough to keep him at a decent school?" the Marquis asked.

"No, of course not!" Rowena answered. "I should not expect those sort of fees even from someone like yourself. But I am saving up, and I thought that when you leave and there is not so much to do I might try to earn a little money of my own."

"How do you contemplate doing that?" the Marquis enquired.

"It is really due to you that I thought of it," Rowena confessed. "We had so much fruit that I have bottled and made jam of what was left over."

"Very sensible – and frugal."

"I thought it would keep us through the winter without having to buy any more," Rowena said. "Then last week the Vicar's wife asked me if I would give a pot for the Vicarage Bazaar. I gave her two, one of peaches and one of green-gages. They actually sold at a shilling each!"

Rowena's voice was quite elated and her eyes were shining as she went on:

"A shilling! And she said she could have sold dozens more pots if she had had them."

The Marquis was watching her as he prompted:

"Go on!"

"The orchard is overgrown, the fruit is not very big, probably because the trees are so old. But there are plenty of damsons and quinces, and later there will be apples. If I could bottle and make jams of those the way Mama showed me from a special recipe, I think they would sell."

Her voice died away as she looked at the Marquis as if waiting for his verdict.

His eyes were on her face as he said:

"I wonder if in a few years time you will feel excited as you are now at the thought of receiving a shilling for a pot of jam."

"It might not be so much when it is not for charity," Rowena said.

"No of course not," he agreed.

She saw from the twinkle in his eyes that he was laughing.

"You are amused," she said hotly. "I know it sounds foolish to you, but it is Mark's whole future."

"I am not laughing at your ambitions, Rowena," the Marquis said. "I think they are admirable. What I am really doing, I think, is envying your enthusiasm. It is a long time since I have been excited or enthusiastic about anything."

"Except your old family tree!" Rowena flashed.

"I stand corrected," he agreed. "My old family tree, as you call it, certainly does excite me, but not to the extent that you are thrilled by the thought of a pot of damson jam."

"It is no use talking to you," she said angrily. "All I am asking you is to help me by giving me the fees you intend to pay Papa, that is, if you do intend to pay him."

"I have many faults," the Marquis replied, "but I assure you that I pay my debts and promptly!"

"Then I am very glad to hear it," Rowena said, "and I only hope that you will give Papa what he deserves."

"I had thought that perhaps a fee of 100 guineas would be acceptable," the Marquis replied.

Rowena's eyes widened and she stared at him in astonishment.

"W . what did you . . say?"

"I said 100 guineas. I consider that is what your father's services are worth."

"You . . are not . . joking?"

"No, I promise you I am entirely serious."

She stared at him for a moment. Then as his eyes met hers she turned away.

"We could not possibly accept so much!"

"I was going to add a quarter of that amount for the quite exceptional nursing I have received."

Rowena drew in her breath and her chin went up.

"I was not asking for charity, My Lord."

"I do not consider it charity," the Marquis replied. "Sir George informed me that if I had been taken the ten miles to my house after the accident the result might have been disastrous."

"That is not the point," Rowena said. "Country physicians, as you well know, do not command large fees."

"You asked me to give your father what I considered he was worth."

"But I think that is too much."

"Do you think you are qualified to judge the value I put on my life?"

"It is not .. that," Rowena said hesitatingly, "it is just that when I asked you to give me the .. fee you would have paid to Papa, I was thinking .. that if you were very .. generous it might be as much as .. twenty guineas."

"I have a rather higher estimate of my value than that."

"That is not what I am .. trying to say."

"I am well aware of what you are trying to say, Rowena," the Marquis answered, "and I assure you I intend to pay your father exactly what I wish without any interference on your part. If you will not accept the money, then of course I can quite easily give it to him direct. I am sure he will find an immediate use for it."

"You are blackmailing me," Rowena protested.

"And why not?" the Marquis enquired. "When I am strong enough to stand up for myself, invariably I get my own way."

"I can well believe that is true," Rowena snapped, "and it is very bad for you."

The Marquis laughed.

"Like all women you wish me to kow-tow to your sex and do as I am told, in which case you will be very disappointed."

Rowena rose.

"Please be sensible for a moment," she begged. "It is very kind of you .. very .. very kind to offer to pay Papa the enormous sum you have just suggested. But I feel you would not have made it so large had I not told you before that it was for Mark. We would be very content and very grateful indeed for half that sum."

"Are you still opposing me, Rowena?" the Marquis asked. "I have just told you that I always get my own way, and I especially wish to do so where you are concerned."

"But .. why?"

"That is something I intend to tell you in detail on another occasion," the Marquis replied.

There was a meaning behind his words she did not understand.

When she looked at him in perplexity and met his eyes, she felt that he was telling her something. There was also something forceful both in his expression and in the line of his lips.

Quite suddenly she felt very young, very inexperienced and vulnerable.

She said the first words that came into her mind.

"I do not .. know what to .. say .. My Lord."

"Then why say anything, Rowena?" the Marquis asked. "Just leave everything to me."

CHAPTER THREE

Looking at the Marquis sitting at the end of the Dining-Room table Rowena thought that he appeared more impressive and more overpowering than she had ever imagined he could be.

There was something very different in seeing him dressed in his elegant evening-clothes instead of the night-shirt to which she had grown accustomed.

Now in the small oak-beamed Dining-Room he appeared almost like a being from another world.

For the last few days he had been allowed first to sit up in his bed-room, then rather unsteadily to come downstairs for an hour or so.

She had known that the effort tired him and she had been concerned with him more as a patient than as a man.

But now there seemed to be no more need for concern, and she had the feeling that when he left the house and returned home to-morrow she would never see him again.

"I shall always remember him like this," she told herself, "sitting back in a high-back chair talking to the family with an amused twist to his lips."

She was never quite certain whether he was teasing or mocking them; but where she herself was concerned she was certain it was the latter.

And yet no-one could be more charming, no-one indeed more gracious.

This evening before dinner he had given the family presents which he said was an expression of his gratitude for having been their guest for so long.

For Dr. Winsford there had been a new microscope which

had delighted him, for Hermione an expensive box of paints, brushes and drawing blocks which had left her speechless.

"I will draw you a beautiful picture," she told the Marquis, "but I am afraid it will never rival the manuscripts of your family tree."

"I shall look forward to receiving it," he answered.

Hermione had stared at her paint-box as if it could hardly be real.

Lotty too was in ecstasies over a doll which had a complete wardrobe including a gown trimmed with real lace.

For Mark the Marquis had chosen, or rather Rowena suspected Mr. Ashburn had done the shopping, a riding-whip with a silver band on which his initials were engraved.

There was a noisy excitement in the Sitting-Room as the family opened their gifts and only when everything had been admired and examined over a dozen times did Hermione say inquisitively:

"Have you not a present for Rowena, My Lord? After all, she has done more for you than any of us."

"I am aware of that," the Marquis replied in his deep voice. "But Rowena's present is not yet ready."

Hermione was satisfied with the explanation, but Rowena wondered with some curiosity what it could be.

She had noticed that she had been left out and had felt a little piqued, thinking that the Marquis perhaps was punishing her for the times when she had duelled with him on so many subjects.

But now quite unexpectedly she felt a warm wave of happiness sweep over her because she had not been forgotten.

The dinner, which was the first the Marquis had attended and also was to be his last, was very special.

Not only had Mrs. Hanson excelled herself in cooking what she declared were "His Lordship's Favourite dishes", but Mr. Ashburn had brought with him this morning pâtés from Swayneling Park besides a variety of delectable sweetmeats for dessert.

Lotty had not been allowed to stay up for dinner, but a dish of the creams, jellies and chocolate fingers had been taken up to her in the Nursery after she had gone to bed.

"I wish the Marquis was not leaving," she said with a deep sigh as she licked her sticky fingers.

"We will have to go back to plain, simple fare," Rowena said as if she was speaking to herself, "but it will be better for us."

"I like the things he gives us," Lotty said stoutly, "and I like him! He is very, very nice – I shall marry him when I grow up!"

Rowena laughed but it was a sound that had not much humour in it.

"Hermione wants to marry him now," Lotty went on. "She was at her desk yesterday, and I looked over her shoulder. She had written: 'I love him!' 'I love him!' all down the page!"

"You should not read things which were not meant for your eyes," Rowena admonished automatically, but she was thinking that she had been right. It was a very good thing the Marquis was leaving!

He would go back to his own world in which he was so important, and if they ever heard from him again she would be very surprised.

She could not help knowing all the same that she would search for his name in the Social column of the *Morning Post* which her father took every day. She supposed also that locally they would enjoy a reflected glory because the Marquis stayed with them for so long.

Perhaps, she thought, some of the County families who had been far too grand to patronise Dr. Winsford in the past would now make use of his services.

Whatever the reason she would welcome them, because they could pay the fees that would go towards Mark's schooling.

The Marquis had given her the 100 guineas this morning and she had taken the cheque from him, although something within herself resented the fact that they could not afford to refuse it.

She wished they could tell the Marquis that his money

was not important .. but what was the point of wishing?

They needed the money desperately and Rowena was obliged to force the words of thanks to her lips.

The Marquis had listened to her, an expression on his face that she did not understand. Then he had said:

"Forget it! Forget your resentment! Forget that you feel yourself forced to accept my munificence! Enjoy feeling that you are rich, at least for a little while."

She raised her eyes to his, then said impulsively:

"I am not really ungrateful. You have been very kind and very generous, and if I can get Mark into a decent school it will all be due to you."

"I intend to talk about that to your father."

"Why?" Rowena asked.

He had not answered and she thought later that perhaps he considered her curiosity was impertinent.

But she told herself that someone as important as the Marquis was doubtless a patron of quite a number of schools and his knowledge and experience would be worth listening to.

Although she told herself it was a good thing that the Marquis was leaving, and it was absurd to make a fuss because he was dining downstairs for the first time, Rowena took more trouble than usual over her appearance.

She had only two gowns which she wore in the evenings. One had belonged to her mother and was of velvet which she wore in the winter, and another for the summer which was of muslin.

She had made it herself and it was in fact of the cheapest material that could be purchased in the adjacent town.

The colour matched the blue of her eyes and although she chided herself for being extravagant she had bought in the village shop a few yards of ribbon to replace the original trimming and give the gown a new look.

Rowena owned no jewellery, but before she went up to change for dinner she walked into the garden and picked two white rose-buds.

When she pinned them between her breasts, she not only felt they made her look a little smarter, but they also gave her a fragrance which somehow enhanced the festivities of the evening.

She was sure the Marquis thought the style in which she arranged her hair was old-fashioned, but she brushed its pale fairness until it shone and she noted with amusement that Hermione wore a new pink ribbon tied coquettishly in a bow.

Rowena suspected that she must have bought this in the village when she went to her lessons with the retired Governess who lived in a small cottage at the far end of it.

She very much doubted if Hermione had the money to pay for her purchase and was certain the bill would arrive after the Marquis had left.

'We have done our best to entertain him,' she thought as they sat round the dinner-table.

She wondered if, when he was surrounded with the elegance and gaiety of his own friends, whether he would laugh at their feeble efforts.

She did not know why she suspected that the Marquis must always be disparaging them, but it was impossible not to feel the contrast he created perhaps without meaning to.

She said very little during dinner. All the time she was acutely conscious of him and thought it would be impossible ever again to find a man who was so handsome and attractive.

There was no doubt that he was doing everything possible to make his last meal in their house a memorable one.

There was champagne to drink, and while Rowena kept a sharp eye on Hermione and Mark to see they did not drink too much she could not help being aware that the golden wine made everybody a little more relaxed.

It was easier to laugh and to accept the Marquis as one of themselves rather than as their awe-inspiring benefactor.

When Johnson, who was waiting at table, filled his Master's glass again, the Marquis raised it in his hand.

"I am going to drink a toast," he said, "first to Dr. Winsford, to whom I shall always be eternally grateful not only for saving my life, but also for making me so welcome in his house, and secondly to my very capable and very lovely nurse – Rowena!"

His words took Rowena by surprise; she felt the colour spring into her face and at the same time was annoyed by her own confusion.

The Marquis turned to the other side of the table and saw Hermione looking at him with adoring eyes.

"To a future artist," he said, "who I suspect will always look more attractive than anything she can draw, and to an equestrian who I hope one day will find mounts worthy of his horsemanship."

Mark and Hermione were delighted and as in response they drank what remained in their own glasses, Rowena rose to her feet.

"I think, Papa, we should leave His Lordship and you to your port."

"I cannot stay long," Dr. Winsford said with a hasty glance at the grandfather clock. "I have two calls to make this evening."

"Oh, Papa!" Rowena said reproachfully.

"You must forgive me," the Doctor said to the Marquis. "But my patients are expecting me, and I would not wish to disappoint them."

"Of course not," the Marquis agreed.

The Doctor glanced at his younger daughter.

"I should be grateful if you would come with me, Hermione," he said. "You know there is nowhere safe to leave Dobbin outside the Blakes's house. The last time I called there, he had wandered a quarter-of-a-mile up the road before I could catch him again."

"I will drive you," Hermione said with just a wistful glance at the Marquis.

As if he understood what she was feeling, he said:

"If I have gone to bed before you return, Hermione, come

and say good-bye to me before you leave for your lessons to-morrow morning."

"I will do that," Hermione replied, "and I expect I will sit up half the night using my wonderful paint-box."

The Marquis had risen to his feet.

Hermione seemed to hesitate for a moment, then she said:

"Thank you so very much, I am so grateful!" and flung her arms around his neck.

It was the action of a child as she kissed his cheek, but Rowena felt a strange feeling within herself that she could not explain as she walked towards the door followed by Mark.

"Do you think I could have a last ride on the Marquis's horse before he leaves to-morrow morning?" he asked her in a conspiratorial tone. "I would like to try out my new whip."

"I cannot think, if the Marquis is collected in his Phaeton, that his grooms will wish to take the horses from between the shafts," Rowena replied. "But if Mr. Ashburn comes over, which I am sure he will, perhaps you can ask him if you can ride the horse which is drawing the Landau."

She paused a moment, then she said:

"Unless the Marquis is attended by out-riders."

"It is not likely as he is going such a short distance," Mark replied.

"No, of course not," Rowena agreed, "so we will just have to see what can be done."

She knew he was longing to ride carrying his new whip. At the same time she would rather he did not tire out Dobbin, who was the only mode of transport available for her father.

"You had better go to your room now," she said. "I am sure you have some home-work to do. The Vicar complained last week that you had been rather careless about it."

"I was too busy riding," Mark said with a grin, then his face fell. "It is going to be pretty dull here when the Marquis has gone, is it not?"

"I was afraid you would feel like that," Rowena answered,

"but there is nothing we can do about it, as you well know."

"No, of course not," Mark said with an effort at appearing grown-up. "We have been jolly lucky to have him so long."

He clattered up the stairs towards his own room and Rowena walked into the Drawing-Room where her mother had always sat.

It was very simply furnished but it was in good taste, and the long French windows opening out on to the garden gave the room an elegance that was not obvious in other parts of the house.

Rowena walked to an open window now and stood looking out on the un-kept garden.

It might be untidy because neither she nor her father ever had time to work in it but the roses grew in wild profusion and there was honeysuckle and purple wistaria climbing along the terrace.

The sun was going down and the sky was crimson.

" 'Red sky at night, shepherds' delight'," Rowena quoted to herself.

It would be a pleasant day for the Marquis to go home to-morrow and she thought he would welcome the opportunity of driving his Phaeton which he had been unable to do since his accident.

She imagined how distinguished he would look with his tall hat on the side of his dark head.

He would drive away, she thought, and that would be the end of the chapter where they were concerned.

She was certain they would never again have such a distinguished patient or the spare room such an unusual occupant.

She felt that he had not only brought new ideas into the house but had given her new feelings and emotions that had never been awakened within her before.

She could not explain even to herself what they were; she only knew they were there and that in some ways she was a different person from what she had been before the Marquis arrived.

"I am imagining things," she told herself, then turned her head as the door opened and Hermione came in.

She had put on a bonnet because she was to accompany her father, and carried a white shawl over her arm.

"I cannot think why I have to go with Papa," she grumbled. "I would much rather stay here with the Marquis."

"You could not refuse," Rowena said.

"No, of course not," Hermione agreed. "But I cannot think why Papa has to work so hard. It is ridiculous to have to go out to-night of all nights!"

"You know Papa would never shirk his duty, even if he would rather stay and talk to the Marquis," Rowena said gently.

"He is so wonderful, is he not?" Hermione said in a low voice but she was not speaking of her father.

"He has been very kind," Rowena said somewhat stiffly.

"You will have to help me think of what I can draw and paint for him," Hermione said. "If only I could do something like those wonderful paintings he has on his family tree."

"You must think of something original," Rowena answered, "and not try to copy someone else."

"I will think of something," Hermione said.

She gave a little sigh.

"It will be more difficult when he is not here to talk to me and give me ideas. I have had lots and lots of new ideas since he has been in the house."

Rowena prevented herself from saying she felt the same. Then there was the sound of voices in the hall and Hermione ran across the room.

"I am going now," Rowena heard her father say.

"I am ready, Papa."

"Good-night, My Lord," Dr. Winsford was saying to the Marquis. "Do not stay up too late, I would not wish you to become over-tired."

"I will try not to be that," the Marquis replied.

63

There was the sound of footsteps, then the front door banged.

Rowena stood at the window but she had the feeling that she was holding her breath.

The Marquis came into the Drawing-Room and closed the door behind him.

Rowena did not turn her head as he walked slowly across the room towards her.

He stopped as he reached her and his eyes were on her profile silhouetted against the evening sky.

"This leaves just you and me, Rowena," he said quietly.

She turned her eyes slowly towards his, conscious that her heart was fluttering in a most unaccountable manner as the Marquis drew something from the pocket of his coat.

"I have your present for you," he said, "but I wanted to give it to you alone."

He put a small box into her hand as he spoke.

She took it from him, conscious as she did so that standing close beside her he was very tall and large, and it was impossible to look at him again.

"Open it!" the Marquis said.

Rowena was aware that she was staring at the box in her hand. She obeyed him.

Inside was a heart-shaped pendant made of turquoises surrounded by diamonds.

"Is this . . for me?" she asked hardly above a whisper.

"A very small expression of my thanks for all you have done for me, Rowena."

"It is . . lovely . . quite lovely!" she exclaimed, "but you should not . ."

She stopped, aware although she was not looking at his lips that the Marquis was smiling.

"Are you once again going to tell me what I should or should not do?" he asked. "You have been very dictatorial, Rowena, and I shall find it difficult to know how to behave without so many strictures to guide me."

"It was for your own . . good," Rowena said faintly.

"I am aware of that," he replied, "and yet I cannot help feeling that you were perhaps rather pleased to have me at your mercy."

She did not answer that and after a moment he said:

"I have never forgotten how gentle your voice was when I was really ill, or how soft your arm felt when you lifted my head."

It was almost as if he spoke to music and Rowena felt her whole body respond to the note in his voice.

She was still staring at the pendant as if she could not believe it was real. She had never possessed anything so lovely or so valuable, and yet there was something more than that.

"I chose that particular shape," the Marquis said quietly, "because it is symbolic."

She looked up at him, and was startled by the expression in his eyes.

He was very near to her, and yet she could not move and having once looked at him could not look away.

"You hold my heart in your hands, Rowena," the Marquis said. "Does that mean anything to you?"

"I do not .. think I .. understand," she managed to murmur, finding it almost impossible to force the words from between her lips.

"Then shall I make it a little clearer?" the Marquis asked, "and also thank you as I wish to do?"

His arms went round her, and almost before she could be aware of what was happening his lips came down on hers.

For a moment she was too surprised to feel anything but sheer astonishment. Then she realised that his mouth held hers captive and she could neither move nor think.

His lips were hard against the softness of hers, and something warm and wonderful seemed to rise within her and move up through her body towards him.

It was a feeling so lovely, so perfect, that she knew it was everything she had longed for in life and had never known.

It was part of the sun-set and the fragrance of the roses; it

65

was the Marquis and everything she felt about him, and so much more.

He drew her a little closer and now she felt she was no longer herself but a part of him, of his elegance and distinction and even his overpowering superiority against which she had fought so ineffectively.

The pressure of his lips increased and almost like a streak of lightning a wonder such as she had never dreamed possible seemed to shoot through her body from her lips to her soul.

It was so perfect, so exquisite and at the same time a rapture so indescribable that instinctively Rowena reached out to hold on to the Marquis lest she should lose something which seemed to come from the Divine.

He raised his head.

"You are so lovely!" he said. "So unbelievably beautiful! When I first saw you I felt I must be delirious."

It was impossible for Rowena to answer him. She could only look up at him, her eyes shining, her lips parted and trembling a little from his kiss and the emotion he had evoked in her.

"I love you!" the Marquis said, "and I know now that you love me."

He pulled her almost roughly closer to him.

"But not as much as I will make you love me," he said. "Oh, my darling, you are so sweet and so innocent. I had no idea that anyone like you could exist in the world."

His lips were on hers again and now he was kissing her fiercely, demandingly, almost as if he would conquer her to make sure she was his.

Only after what seemed to Rowena to be a very long time was she free again.

Now slowly, because it was difficult to speak, because she felt dazed and bewildered by what had happened she murmured:

"I .. love you .. I know now .. that what I .. felt for you .. was love!"

"But you fought against it," the Marquis said perceptively.

"I did not .. know I loved you," Rowena said. "I only knew that you .. seemed overpowering .. I was afraid of losing my own .. identity."

"You have lost it," he said positively.

She turned her face to hide it against his shoulder, overwhelmed by her own feelings, fascinated, dazzled and at the same time feeling as if her whole being had come alive so that it vibrated to his.

His fingers went under her chin to turn her face up towards his.

"Do you know how beautiful you are?" he asked. "How could any woman be so lovely or have eyes that are not human, but are part of the sky?"

He kissed them as he spoke, then his lips touched Rowena's straight little nose before once again he sought her mouth.

He kissed her until she felt as if the garden swum dizzily around them, and the house was falling!

Then the Marquis drew her back into the Drawing-Room.

"Let us sit down, my darling," he said. "I want to talk to you."

"I .. I did not .. know that love was like .. this," Rowena said a little incoherently.

"Like what?" he asked.

"So wonderful .. so perfect. When you kissed me .. we seemed to be .. alone in the sky where there is only .. music."

"That is what I want," the Marquis said, "that we should be alone, just you and I Rowena, so that I can teach you, my precious, about love."

"I suppose because I have never been .. in love before .. I did not .. realise that was what I felt for you," she whispered.

"And you will never be in love again," the Marquis said.

"You belong to me, Rowena, and I shall be very jealous if another man so much as speaks to you."

Looking at her face again he said:

"I feel like an explorer who finds an unknown, unlisted flower on the summit of a mountain and knows he has discovered a treasure which the world has never known."

He laughed.

"You are making me poetical, Rowena, which is something I have never been."

She drew in her breath.

"Is it true .. really true that you .. love me?"

The question was child-like.

"It is true!" he answered. "I have been loving you for days. I felt when you went out of my room that you took the light with you, and I would lie awake at night wishing I was ill again so that you would be beside me and I could hear your voice and feel you touch me."

"When you were ill," Rowena said, "I felt that you were like a child who needed me as Lotty or Mark might do. But to-night .."

She paused.

"What about to-night?" the Marquis asked.

"You are so much a .. man that I am .. afraid."

"Afraid?" he questioned.

"You are different .. and I know that you are .. going away."

"And you wanted me!"

There was a wealth of meaning behind the word 'want' and Rowena felt a little quiver run through her. But she did not answer him and after a moment the Marquis said:

"I will teach you to want me as I want you, and we will not lie awake at night, my darling heart, alone and feeling lonely."

He kissed her again and this time there was a fire on his lips which seemed to Rowena to awaken a flickering flame deep down in her body.

She could not understand it, but it was very strange and

wonderful, and although she was a little afraid she knew it was what he wished her to feel.

The Marquis kissed the corners of her mouth and the dimples in her cheeks, then he bent his head to kiss the softness of her neck and to give her a strange sensation that was diffcrent to what she had felt before. It was even, she thought, more wonderful.

"I love you!" he said again. "It is difficult to think of anything else because I love you and want you with me, both by day and by night, and it is impossible, my precious one, to think of anything but you."

"But .. you are leaving .. tomorrow."

The Marquis raised his head and sat up a little straighter, but his arms were still around her.

"I must go home, as it is arranged," he said, "but we have to make plans so that we can be together without upsetting your father."

"It will upset him to lose me," Rowena agreed, "but it was inevitable that it should happen one day."

She smiled a little shyly and went on:

"I have thought about it .. not that I imagined I would .. love you .. but because I could not leave the children with no-one to look after them."

"No, of course not," the Marquis agreed.

"I am certain .. although I have never mentioned it to her .. that Miss Graham, who teaches Hermione, would be only too pleased to move in here. Her cottage is very small and very damp which gives her rheumatism in the winter. She thinks Papa is wonderful and would look after him."

"Then that makes it very easy," the Marquis said.

"You are .. certain .. quite certain that you want me?"

"Do you really need me to answer that very foolish question?" he enquired.

But there was no need for words as he kissed her and Rowena felt the urgency behind his lips and the fire which seemed to unite them both.

For a moment she felt as if there were flames so intense

and so consuming that she might lose her whole identity in them. Then the Marquis's lips became less fierce and possessive and instead were tender and caressing.

"You are very young," he said softly, "I would not wish to frighten you."

"I am .. not frightened," Rowena replied. "It is all so .. perfect .. so wonderful! Are you sure I am not dreaming?"

"If you are, then I am dreaming too."

He laid his cheek against hers as he went on:

"Could anyone be so soft and sweet and at the same time excite me to the edge of madness? Oh, my darling, how long have I to wait until we can be together?"

"You must not do anything which is bad for you," Rowena said quickly. "You must remember that you will not be really well for some time. You must take things easily."

"You call this easy?" the Marquis asked with laughter in his voice.

"It is .. marvellous! Perfect!" Rowena replied; "but loving may make you tired."

"I suspect that it will," the Marquis answered, "but a different sort of tiredness and one which you will find can be very wonderful, my sweet!"

Rowena did not understand what he meant but she was too happy to want to ask questions.

The mere fact that the Marquis's arms were around her and his lips were near to hers was too much of a miracle for her to be able to think straight.

All she wanted was that he should go on kissing her and arousing within her those ecstatic rapturous emotions which she had not known she was capable of feeling.

She put her head against his shoulder with a little sigh. "I want to take care of you. Even though you are so important, I think perhaps you need me."

"I need you for a thousand different reasons," the Marquis said. "Most of all I want you because you are mine, you are a part of me, and it is impossible to think of myself in the future without you."

"That is what I want you to .. feel," Rowena replied, "but you have known so many beautiful women who I am sure have been alluring and exciting. Supposing, after a little while I begin to .. bore you?"

"I know you will never do that," the Marquis said, "but whatever happens, my precious, I shall always look after you, and you shall never regret that you have given me yourself."

He kissed her forehead, then he said:

"Now in case your father returns sooner than we expected we must make plans, you and I. I have been thinking about this."

"About us?" Rowena enquired.

"I have thought of nothing else these last few days," he answered, "and I think the best thing will be for you to tell your father that I have arranged for you to come to London as a companion to one of my relations."

Rowena was very still.

It was almost as if her whole body which was close against the Marquis had become so rigid that it had turned into stone.

In a voice she could not recognise as her own she asked:

"Wh .. what are you .. saying to me?"

"I am trying to find a plausible explanation for your going to London," the Marquis replied. "There will of course, be no relative, but I have a house in Chelsea, a very attractive little house, which is ready for you now. There will be two servants to look after you, and we will be together at every possible moment, that I promise you!"

With what seemed to be a superhuman effort Rowena moved from the circle of his arms.

"I .. I still do not .. understand," she said and now there was a piteous note in her voice.

The Marquis looked down into her eyes, then he rose to his feet.

"I did not mean to mislead you," he said. "I thought you would realise."

71

"I .. I .. thought .." Rowena began.

He walked across the room to stand as she had done, leaning against the lintel of the window looking out into the garden.

"This is more difficult than I anticipated," he said after a moment. "I suppose I forgot how young and innocent you are, how unversed in the ways of the world."

Sitting on the sofa Rowena clasped her hands together. They were very cold.

"Are you .. saying .. are you .. telling me that you .. do not love me?"

"No, of course I am not saying that," the Marquis replied. "I love you as I swear to you I have never loved a woman before, but I cannot offer you marriage."

He spoke very quietly, and yet to Rowena his words seemed to ring out in the Drawing-Room and echo round its walls.

She felt as if her whole body became as cold as her fingers and there was a block of ice in her heart.

"Then what .. are you saying?" she murmured.

"I am asking you to be with me because I love you and I think you love me," the Marquis answered. "We can be happy together, very, very happy, Rowena!"

He looked towards her as he spoke, but her eyes were downcast, looking at her interlocked fingers.

She looked very young, little more than a child, and his voice was gentle as he said:

"I should have explained to you before that marriage and love in the world in which I live are two very different things. I know what you are feeling, Rowena, and you must forgive me for hurting you. I did not intend to do so."

Still she did not speak and after a moment's pause he continued:

"You have seen my family tree, you know what I feel about my ancestors. To me it is as though I was born with a sacred trust – a duty, if you like, to carry on the family name."

He drew a deep breath before he continued:

"There is no question of personal feelings where marriage is concerned. It is a question of noble blood being matched with noble blood, of putting the family first and being true to one's inheritance."

The Marquis moved back towards Rowena as he said:

"I want you to understand, my darling, that what I feel for you is something quite apart from anything I shall feel for my wife, when I have one. In fact I do not intend to marry for years, and when I do it will be a *mariage de convenance* such as are arranged in France."

He reached the sofa and after a moment's pause sat down beside Rowena.

He did not touch her but a little quiver shook her although her eyes remained on her hands.

"In the meantime," the Marquis continued, "we can be happy together. I will settle money on you, Rowena, so that you will never want again in the whole of your life. You will be mine in everything but name and I believe, because we both love each other, you will find that is of no consequence. What is important to both of us will be our love."

"A love that is . . wrong and . . wicked!"

She spoke beneath her breath, and yet he could hear the words distinctly.

"Who is to say what is wrong, or what is wicked?" the Marquis asked. "What we feel for each other could never be anything but good and perfect."

He put out his hand as he spoke to cover hers, felt how cold they were, and knew that she trembled because he touched her.

"You love me," he said. "You love me in a way that you have never loved anyone before. I am the first man who has kissed you and you are mine – mine completely and absolutely. Try to understand, Rowena, that I will give you everything in the world, everything you want, and we will know a happiness which is vouchsafed to few people as fortunate as we are."

"B . but it would be . . wrong."

"Nothing can be wrong as long as we do not hurt people," the Marquis replied. "I have already explained to you that your father will not know, nor will Hermione have the slightest idea that you are not employed in London and thus able to send them plenty of money. They can have the luxuries they have never been able to afford in the past."

"If they learnt that I had . . lied to them . . what do you imagine they would . . think?" Rowena asked.

"There is no reason why they should know," the Marquis replied. "We are both intelligent people and we will make quite certain there is no gossip. No-one will know – that I promise you!"

"But *I* should know."

There was a pain in the words that was inescapable and at the same time she raised her head and straightened her back.

"*I* should know," she repeated, "and should be ashamed to face my own family!"

She moved as she spoke and the Marquis's hands fell away from hers.

She stood in front of the mantelpiece and drew in her breath almost as if she needed to resuscitate herself before she could speak. Then she said slowly and distinctly:

"I love you. I think I shall always love you . . but I cannot . . do as you . . ask."

"Why not?" the Marquis asked. "Why should you deny yourself and me what both of us long and crave for, not only with our bodies, Rowena, but also with our hearts and minds?"

His eyes were on her face as he went on:

"You are letting conventional prejudices blind you to the fact that a love such as we have for each other is very rare and comes once in a life-time. You say you love me, and I think that is true, and I love you overwhelmingly. I know you want me. I cannot live without you. Can you refuse me just because you are setting your sights on some impossible goal?"

"Yes, I can!" Rowena said. "I cannot believe that I could mean anything to you beyond a passing amusement, an interest that would die as quickly as it came to life. That is not love, My Lord .. not *real* love!"

"You are talking nonsense about a matter of which you know nothing!" the Marquis retorted. "I do love you, Rowena. I love you with all my heart. Just because I cannot marry you – which is a very different thing – that does not mean to say that I am not prepared to devote my whole life to you – I am! Why should you ask for more?"

"What you are really saying," Rowena said, and now there was a touch of anger in her voice, "is how dare I ask for more! I .. an unimportant Doctor's daughter ought to be overwhelmed that a nobleman such as yourself should condescend to notice her, let alone love her! Well, My Lord, I *do* dare! I dare to tell you that the love you offer is not good enough for me. I am sorry, but there is no more to be said on the matter."

She turned towards the door, but before she could reach it the Marquis had risen to his feet.

He caught her once again in his arms and pulled her roughly against him. Then he kissed her fiercely, passionately and with a violence that was almost brutal.

At first his lips hurt her almost intolerably; then although she tried to prevent it, although she attempted to struggle against him, the lightning shot through her as it had done before and she felt herself grow limp against him.

His kisses became more gentle, but at the same time more possessive.

She felt as if he demanded not only her body but her very soul and attempted to draw it from her and make it his.

She knew he was striking at her resistance, undermining her opposition, compelling her with every nerve and sinew to surrender herself completely and absolutely to what he demanded.

For a moment the wonder of what he made her feel, the ecstasy which was so intense as to blot out thought, made it impossible to move, but only to feel.

Then she fought against him frantically, and taken by surprise he loosened his hold on her and she was free.

She did not speak to him because it would have been impossible.

She only pulled open the door and ran away before he could stop her, knowing as she stumbled up the stairs that she was blinded by the tears that had begun to run tempestuously down her face.

CHAPTER FOUR

Coming back from the village Rowena turned into the small, unkept drive which led up to the house and saw with a sudden constriction of her heart that there was a Phaeton standing outside the front door.

There was no need to question who owned the black and yellow vehicle with its shining silver accoutrements and the four magnificent horses pulling it.

A groom, with a cockaded top-hat and yellow turn-overs on his boots was standing at the horses' heads and Rowena knew that the Marquis would be inside the house.

It was four days since he had left for Swayneling Park and she had thought as he drove away that she would never see him again.

Not that she wanted to, she told herself fiercely. She had even decided that she would not say good-bye to him, but he had been too clever for her.

After a sleepless night when she had cried intermittently with an abandonment and a despair she had not known since she was a small child, with the dawn she had felt pride come to her rescue.

She told herself that however deeply she was wounded, however unhappy she would be, she would not allow the Marquis the satisfaction of knowing that he had completely annihilated her and she could no longer stand up to him.

She had a feeling that he would not be defeated easily and that somehow he would try to persuade her to agree to what he wanted.

There was an obstinacy about him which was un-mistakable and what she knew was an iron determination to have his own way.

But she was resolved, as she had never been resolved before, that though he might break her heart she would never agree to become his mistress.

"I love him! I love him!" she had sobbed into her pillow.

But even the new, ecstatic emotions he had aroused in her did not prevent her from recognising what was right and what was wrong, or knowing that her mother would have been shocked and horrified by what he had suggested.

Although she tried to be practical, Rowena had all her life been idealistic and romantic.

Because her father and mother had been so happy, because they lived in a world where nothing mattered except their love for each other, Rowena had always imagined that one day she would find a man for whom she would feel the same.

She had been conscious that her mother's love for her father was a very moving and very vital thing.

Mrs. Winsford would listen for the first sound of the wheels coming up the drive, and if it was the time she was expecting him to return she would drop everything she was doing and run to the front door to greet him on the steps as he alighted from his gig.

Then his arms would go round her and locked together they would move into the house to kiss in the hall with a tenderness that was unmistakable.

"You are so beautiful, my dearest one!" Rowena heard her father say once, "that I can never look at you without thinking I am the most fortunate of men."

He had laughed and added:

"People think I am poor, but actually I own the most precious treasure in the whole world – and that is you!"

As she became adolescent and began to think about love, Rowena had hoped that one day a man would look at her as her father looked at her mother and his voice would deepen when he spoke to her.

She had not imagined that love would come to her in the

shape of anyone so magnificent, so outstanding in fact unique as the Marquis.

But now she told herself it was inevitable that living the restricted, quiet life she had lived for nineteen years she would fall overwhelmingly and hopelessly in love with him.

"I might have know that what he felt for me was not love but something quite different," she told herself bitterly.

Innocent though she was in many ways, Rowena could not have been a Doctor's daughter and not be aware of the tragedies that happened even in a village as small as Little Powick.

There were girls who found themselves having unwanted babies, married women who were beaten up by their husbands because they had been caught behaving improperly with another man, and a suicide which had left an indelible mark on Rowena's mind.

She had know the girl who died, a pretty, feckless child, for she was little more, whose innocence had attracted the Pub-Keeper, a coarse, rather brutal man, married to a weak wife who had little or no influence over him.

All the village knew that they were meeting down by the river, but no-one was brave enough to interfere and the Vicar was too indolent.

It was a brief and doubtless tempestuous affair with which the Pub-Keeper was soon bored.

He returned to his bawdy friends in the Bar and the girl, who had been swept off her feet by his ardency, drowned herself in the shame of learning that she carried his child.

There was such an uproar in the village and so much unpleasantness was engendered by the tragedy that the Pub-Keeper moved away to another locality and was replaced by a more decent man.

But that, Rowena had thought, did not bring back to life the pathetic victim who, because she had taken her own life, was not even allowed to rest in the village Churchyard.

'If I do what the Marquis wants,' she thought, 'I should be

no better than poor little Bessie, and I might easily finish up the same way.'

She decided the only thing she could do was never to see the Marquis again and she had no intention of saying good-bye to him.

But when the moment came for him to leave he sent Johnson to find her.

Rowena had hidden herself in Mark's room, tidying his clothes, taking a variety of strange objects out of his trouser pockets, and laying on the bed those things which needed mending.

"Ah! Here you are, Miss," Johnson said from the door. "His Lordship would like to say good-bye to you."

Rowena drew in her breath.

"The Doctor is not at home?" she asked.

Johnson shook his head.

"No, Miss. He drove off nearly an hour ago and said good-bye to His Lordship before he left."

Rowena longed to refuse to come downstairs and to send a message to say she was too busy. But she felt that such rudeness would surprise Johnson, and it would also be, the Marquis might think, a score to him.

In the battle between them she would not yield an inch, and she was certain that he would continue to fight her with every weapon at his command.

She could still hear him saying: 'I always get my own way.'

In this instance he was going to be disappointed! And she wanted to make him aware of it.

"I will come down at once," she said to the valet and took a quick glance at her reflection in the mirror.

She was looking very pale and there were lines under her eyes from the tears she had shed and the fact that she had been unable to sleep.

Fiercely, because she would not give the Marquis the satisfaction of seeing how much he had upset her, she rubbed her cheeks until there was some colour in them.

Then holding her chin high she swept downstairs, conscious as she did so that the Marquis was standing in the hall watching her.

She did not look at him as she sank down in a deep curtsey, saying as she did so:

"I am so glad that Your Lordship has a nice day in which to drive home. I am sure my father will have told you to rest on arrival. I am afraid, My Lord, you will find it quite an ordeal having been incapacitated for so long."

Rowena thought with satisfaction that her voice sounded calm and impersonal.

Only as she realised that Johnson had left the hall and they were alone together did she feel her heart flutter uncomfortably.

"I have a great deal to thank you for, Rowena," the Marquis said.

"There is no need for you to say more than you have said already, My Lord," she replied. "I am only glad that my father has been able to restore you to good health."

He took a step nearer to her.

"Rowena!"

She felt herself quiver at the depth in his voice but turned hastily away to walk through the open front door and out on to the steps.

She stared at his Phaeton with its magnificent horses, at the groom holding the reins and a footman waiting to assist his master before he sprang up on to the seat behind.

"I want to talk to you," she heard the Marquis say behind her in a voice that only she could hear.

"Good-bye, My Lord! I wish you a very pleasant journey and good health in the future!"

"*Au revoir*, Rowena," he replied quietly.

Then because it was impossible for him to do otherwise he climbed into the Phaeton.

"Does Your Lordship wish to drive?" Rowena heard the groom ask.

"No, Sam, you tool them for the moment," the Marquis replied.

The groom saluted, the footman sprang up behind and the horses started off.

The Marquis raised his hat, his eyes on Rowena's face, but deliberately she did not look at him.

Only when the Phaeton was almost out of sight did she take a quick glance at his square shoulders and the arrogant carriage of his head and feel the tears come into her eyes.

She walked into the house to slam the door violently behind her.

"It is finished! It is over! That is the end!" she said aloud and wondered why everything seemed so dark and without hope.

In the days that followed Rowena had forced herself to try to keep the Marquis from her mind, and it was only at night that it was impossible not to remember the feelings he had evoked in her when he held her in his arms, and to dream that once again his lips were on hers.

As she had suspected, it was not easy for the family to adjust itself to the normal routine they had known before the Marquis had come to stay.

"I am fed up with this boring food," Hermione had said crossly at luncheon that day.

"It is all we can afford," Rowena retorted sharply, "and the sooner you realise that is the truth the better!"

Hermione groaned.

"If only the Marquis would have another accident or Papa could find another wealthy patient."

"It is all very well to fuss about food," Mark said glumly, "I do not suppose I shall ever have another chance of riding decent horses."

"Stop grumbling – both of you!" Rowena ordered. "And, Mark, if I have another bad report about your lessons from the Vicar I shall speak to Papa. You know how upset he would be to think you are wasting your time."

This was true and it also was the one effective threat that Rowena could hold over the children's heads.

They all loved their father, and because the Doctor was

never angry when they behaved badly but instead was deeply hurt and worried, it was in fact the greatest punishment they could be given.

Mark had mumbled something as he left the Dining-Room, while Hermione had stoically finished her plate of rice-pudding before she said:

"Mark is right. It is horrible now the Marquis has gone, and I believe you miss him, even though you will not say so. You certainly look miserable enough!"

"I am nothing of the sort!" Rowena snapped. "And if you do not hurry to Miss Graham's you will be late. You know as well as I do, Hermione, it is a struggle to pay her fees, small though they are."

"I want to have drawing lessons," Hermione pouted. "Miss Graham cannot even draw a straight line, let alone teach me."

Rowena did not answer and after a moment Hermione continued:

"Not that I expect any sympathy from you. I believe you are jealous because the Marquis gave me such a marvellous present and gave you nothing."

"Hurry up, Hermione, you are going to be late."

Rowena tried to speak quietly and calmly, but perhaps something of what she was feeling showed in her voice, or her face, for quite suddenly Hermione flung her arms around her.

"I am sorry, Rowena," she cried. "I love you, and it was horrid of the Marquis not to give you a present. I will save up and give you something you really want to make up for it."

"Thank you, dearest," Rowena managed to say, then Hermione had gone.

She felt guilty when she thought of the turquoise pendant hidden at the back of the drawer in her bed-room, but she could not speak of it nor could she bear to look at it again.

She considered whether she would return it to the Marquis then she felt that was undignified.

They had often laughed as a family about people who broke off an engagement and sent back each other's letters and presents.

"Thomas Seaton spent a fortune courting Betty," Hermione had related of one broken engagement in the village, "but it all went on chocolates! She can hardly give those back, can she?"

'One day perhaps I will sell the pendant,' Rowena planned, 'and buy something for Hermione or for Mark.'

For the moment she could not open the box in which it reposed, could not bear to look at the heart-shape of the turquoise which the Marquis had said was symbolic.

But now he was here in the house and presumably waiting to see her.

As she walked up the drive, her footsteps growing slower and slower as she neared the house, she tried to think what she should do.

Living in such a small building she could not possibly avoid him for long, and the last thing she wished to do was to arouse any suspicion in the minds of the family that she might have quarrelled with the Marquis.

She knew Hermione and perhaps her father would ask innumerable questions if they thought that anything was wrong.

There was nothing she could tell them, for it would be an intolerable agony to talk about what had happened.

"I will behave normally," Rowena told herself. "He shall not have the satisfaction of driving me into hiding or even thinking that he has made me miserable."

That was a very inadequate word, she thought, to express what she felt.

Despondency, despair were perhaps nearer the mark, or perhaps the real truth was that he had smashed her ideals and destroyed her hope of happiness.

'Any man who comes into my life in the future I am bound to compare with the Marquis,' Rowena thought.

She knew too that it would be impossible for any other

man to arouse in her the same feelings of ecstasy and rapture which the Marquis had done.

That, she was certain, could happen only once in a life-time.

Her mother had said once: "When the right man comes into your life, darling, when you fall in love as I fell in love with your father, you know that it is your destiny and nothing can alter or change it."

Mrs. Winsford had given a deep sigh.

"Your father and I were meant for each other from the very beginning of time, and when we met I knew it was written in the stars that we should love each other until we die."

'That is what I feel for the Marquis,' Rowena told herself, 'but as he does not feel the same about me his destiny can never include me.'

She had reached the Phaeton by this time and the groom at the horses' heads raised his hat.

She saw it was Sam who had come quite a number of times to the house when the Marquis had been ill.

"Good afternoon, Sam," Rowena said. "That is a beautiful team you have there."

"His Lordship's real proud of 'em, Miss," Sam answered, "an' they brought us here quicker to-day than we've ever managed afore, but then His Lordship was a-driving."

The pride in his voice was unmistakable and Rowena smiled at him as she went up the steps and into the house.

The Marquis's tall hat was on a chair in the hall and she hesitated a moment wondering where he would be.

Then to her relief she heard voices coming from her father's Study and knew that he was at home.

She was just about to go upstairs and take off her bonnet when the door opened and her father said:

"I thought I heard your voice, Rowena. We have a visitor!"

"What a surprise!" Rowena exclaimed sarcastically.

She walked into the Study and saw the Marquis standing with his back to the fireplace.

Although she told herself he now meant nothing to her, her heart turned over in a most alarming fashion and it was difficult to breathe.

"Good afternoon, Rowena," the Marquis said. "I was hoping I should see you before I left."

"I must not detain Your Lordship."

"I think, My Lord," Dr. Winsford said, "we must tell Rowena of your generosity. I can hardly believe myself that there is so much kindness in the world."

Rowena glanced sharply at her father.

"What has happened?"

"His Lordship has said, my dear, that he wishes to be responsible for both Mark's schooling and Hermione's. He thinks that Mark is an outstanding boy, as I have always thought myself, and where Hermione is concerned we will be able to ascertain whether she has any real talent for drawing or not."

"I personally think it is just her imagination," Rowena said stiffly.

"We shall find out the truth because His Lordship intends to send her to a Finishing School in Florence where she will have the best teachers that Italy can provide."

'Florence?" Rowena exclaimed.

The word seemed to echo round the Study as her eyes met the Marquis's defiantly.

She was well aware what he was trying to do.

He was trying to manipulate her family into accepting him as she had refused to do.

He was binding them to him, not with bands of steel, but with something far more subtle, far more indefinible.

"I have made enquiries," he said, "and I find that the best Seminary for Young Ladies of Hermione's age is in Florence. In fact one of my nieces will be a pupil there next year, and if Hermione starts this September she will be able to look after her."

"Have you agreed to this, Papa?" Rowena asked in a voice that shook.

"I was at first reluctant to impose on my ex-patient's good nature," Dr. Winsford replied. "But he has in fact convinced me that I must not stand in the way of my children's future."

"I am sure he was very persuasive," Rowena remarked.

"I have of course worried for a long time about Mark's schooling," the Doctor confessed. "The Vicar tells me he has an exceptionally quick mind. In fact everybody who has taught him up to date has said he is very advanced for his age. If, as the Marquis suggests, he goes to Eton, he will have a chance in life which I could never provide for him."

"Eton?" Rowena ejaculated.

Because she felt she needed air she took off her bonnet and walked to the window.

The sun seemed to halo her head with gold but she looked out with blind eyes into the garden.

She was thinking frantically of what she could say, how she could prevent her father from being inveigled into the Marquis's clutches, for that was what it amounted to.

'He is like an octopus,' she thought, 'encircling us all until we will find it impossible to escape.'

"I quite understand that this is somewhat of a shock to you, Rowena," Dr. Winsford said. "You have looked after the family so splendidly since your mother's death, and I cannot think what I could have done without you."

He put his hand on her shoulder.

"But at the same time, my dear, both Hermione and Mark can now receive an education which I could not even dream of giving them."

"Yes .. Papa."

Rowena found it hard to say the words, but she managed to utter them and Dr. Winsford looked relieved, as if he had been afraid she might protest against his decision.

He glanced at the clock on the mantelpiece.

"If Your Lordship will excuse me," he said, "I am already late, and I have a large number of calls to make."

"Of course!" the Marquis replied courteously. "I have spoken, Doctor, of the splendid manner in which you looked after me to a number of my friends in the County. I think you will find in the future there will be many more calls on your time even than you have at the moment."

"It is extremely kind of you, My Lord."

The two men shook hands.

"You certainly look in perfect health," the Doctor said, "but do not do too much too quickly. Remember you had a lucky escape with regard to internal injuries, and a body does not heal itself after that sort of accident within a few days or weeks."

"I promise you I am being as careful as you advised me to be."

"I am glad of that."

"I will return either to-morrow or the next day with the papers we talked about," the Marquis said.

"I shall look forward to seeing you," the Doctor replied.

He went from the room looking happier than he had for a long time and Rowena knew that the Marquis had lifted a heavy burden of worry from his shoulders. At the same time only she knew the explanation of it.

She waited until she heard her father leave the house, then shut the door of the Study and turned to face the Marquis.

"Why can you not leave us alone?" she asked fiercely.

"I have the welfare of your family at heart."

"That is nonsense and you know it!" Rowena said. "They mean nothing to you and you would never have thought of them again if it had not been . ."

She paused finding it difficult to put what she wanted to say into words.

". . . if it had not been for what we feel about each other," the Marquis finished for her. "I love you, Rowena, and I cannot tell you how much I have missed you these last few days."

"I do not wish to hear it, My Lord. There is no point in

discussing either your feelings or mine. I can only beg you to reconsider the offer you have made regarding Hermione and Mark."

"Are you so selfish as to deprive them for purely personal motives?" the Marquis enquired.

"You are trying to get your own way by underhand and despicable methods," Rowena said accusingly, "but you are wasting your time."

"Am I?"

"You certainly are!"

"I find you irresistible when your eyes flash at me," he said, "and you know, Rowena, although you are raging at me, what I want is to hold you in my arms and kiss you again."

She felt a thrill run through her and was furious because she could not prevent it.

"Please go!" she ordered. "You will gain nothing by coming here and talking to me like this. If you gave the family the Bank of England and decorated the house with diamonds I still will not do what you ask of me! What is more, I hate you for trying to blackmail me, because that is what it amounts to."

The Marquis took a step towards her.

"Look at me, Rowena!"

She wanted to refuse, but it was impossible.

Her eyes were drawn irresistibly to his and when their eyes met it was hard to look away.

"I love you!" the Marquis said softly. "I love you, my darling, and you are more beautiful even than I remember. How can you fight against what we feel for each other?"

"What you feel for me," Rowena said, "and what I feel for you are two very different things."

"Are they so very different?" the Marquis enquired.

He came a step nearer and now Rowena knew he would put his arms around her.

If he did so she thought wildly she would be lost.

She wanted the touch of his lips more than she had ever wanted anything in her life.

She wanted to feel the rapture and the wonder which had seemed to transport her into the sky and had been more perfect, more wonderful and more divine than anything she had ever dreamt of or imagined.

"I want you!" the Marquis said and now his voice was deep with passion.

Rowena gave a little cry like that of an animal caught in a trap.

Even as his arms reached out to hold her, she turned and ran, pulling open the door and tearing across the hall and up the stairs as if all the devils of hell were at her heels.

She rushed into her bed-room, locked the door and flung herself down on her bed feeling as if her whole body was throbbing and pulsating because she wanted him more and more with every breath she took.

"Oh, God, help me!" she prayed, and thought in that moment that even God had forsaken her.

*   *   *   *   *

When Doctor Winsford told Hermione and Mark what the Marquis had planned for them they were at first stunned into silence.

"To Florence?" Hermione exclaimed. "Did he really say he was sending me to Florence?"

"To a Finishing School there, where only the élite of Society send their daughters," her father explained. "His Lordship has chosen it because you will have there the best Art Teachers available and that is what he thought you wanted."

"I cannot believe it!" Hermione said. "I never dreamt .. never imagined I would ever leave this village and see the world .. but Florence .. Italy! Oh, Papa, how can I ever thank him?"

"We are all very grateful," the Doctor replied. "At first I felt much embarrassed by his generosity, but he persuaded me to accept for your sakes, and I cannot believe he would do anything that was not right."

"Of course he is right," Hermione said, "and Papa, I will work so hard that you will all be very proud of me."

"I am sure you will, my dear," Dr. Winsford replied.

"But there is one thing I must ask," Hermione said, and it was almost a cry. "What about . . clothes?"

"The Marquis has thought of that too," Dr. Winsford answered. "He told me that his sister, who has a daughter just a little younger than you, will choose you exactly the right gowns and all the other things you require if you will send her your measurements."

"I must be dreaming!" Hermione murmured.

Mark had been rather quiet and now Dr. Winsford said:

"I know how thrilled you will be, Mark, to attend a school with boys of your own age, and Eton, where the Marquis was himself, is undoubtedly the best Public School in England!"

Rowena suddenly felt she could bear no more.

She went into the kitchen to help Mrs. Hanson with the dinner, to find her full of grumbles now that the kitchen-maid had returned to Swayneling Park and she had to do everything herself.

"I'm gettin' too old t' work without help, Miss Rowena," she said, "and that's the truth."

"You will find it less arduous in the future," Rowena replied. "His Lordship is sending Miss Hermione and Master Mark to boarding school."

She could not help the bitterness sounding in her voice as she spoke. Mrs. Hanson merely gave an exclamation of astonishment and then said:

" 'Tis kind of His Lordship – very kind, an' I knows how pleased your dear mother would be, God rest her soul. But I had my suspicions that His Lordship were sweet on you, Miss Rowena, and now I'm a-certain of it!"

"You are mistaken!" Rowena said quickly.

"Not I!" Mrs. Hanson retorted. "I might be deaf, Miss Rowena, but I've got eyes in me head. I knows more about what's going on than people gives me credit for. You mark my words, His Lordship'll be popping the question one of these days, and a finer, more upstanding man t'would be hard to find."

Rowena flounced out of the kitchen, feeling there was no escape from the Marquis wherever she went.

It did not assuage her feelings to find that after his call he had left behind him the usual great hamper of fruit, pâtés, meat and chickens such as they had received during the time he was ill.

"To eat one mouthful would choke me!" Rowena told herself.

Nevertheless when the food came to the table she was forced to eat it because there was nothing else.

She was still very conscious of what she thought of as 'The Marquis's underhand methods of behaviour' when they went up to bed.

All through supper Hermione could talk of nothing but the excitement of going abroad, and her father seemed more relaxed and happy than he had ever been since her mother's death.

Just before the meal was served a knock on the front door was answered by Mark, who had rushed into the Study where the rest of the family were assembled and handed his father a note.

"This has been brought by a slap-up groom," he said excitedly, "riding the most magnificent roan! He is waiting for an answer, Papa."

Dr. Winsford looked at the note in surprise, then opened it and read it carefully.

"Who is it from?" Rowena asked, unable to contain her curiosity.

"It is from General Franklin of Overton House," Dr. Winsford replied.

"General Franklin? We have not heard from the Franklins for years."

"He tells me that he has had such a glowing account of the manner in which I treated the Marquis after an accident that he would wish me in the future to attend him and his entire household. He has asked if I would call on him to-morrow morning."

"How exciting, Papa!" Hermione exclaimed. "Overton House is very impressive. I have seen it from the road and always longed to go to the parties they give."

"The General is asking me to be his medical adviser," the Doctor said. "That does not mean that we shall receive any social recognition, Hermione."

"You never know," Hermione answered irrepressibly. "He might take a fancy to you, Papa, as the Marquis has, from which we would all benefit. Write to him quickly and say that you will be delighted to call to-morrow."

"That is just what I intend to do," Dr. Winsford said, and sat down at his desk.

"Have I any decent writing-paper, Rowena?" he asked.

Rowena got him what he required, but found it impossible to join in the general speculation and excitement over the prospect of a new and wealthy patient.

It was all part of the Marquis's plan to make her change her mind, and once again she compared him to an octopus reaching out his tentacles, making escape from him impossible.

"I hate him!" she told herself.

Yet she felt again the thrill that ran through her when he told her of his love.

. . . . .

The next day, after a restless night in which she was afraid to fall asleep in case she dreamed of him, Rowena came down to breakfast to find that Mark had already had his and gone.

"Master Mark was very early this morning," she said to Mrs. Hanson.

"I thinks he's a-goin' on a picnic, Miss Rowena."

"A picnic?" Rowena asked. "He is doing nothing of the sort! He has lessons with the Vicar at eleven o'clock."

"Well, that's what I thought he means to do," Mrs. Hanson replied. "He asks me to pack some sandwiches in a bag and I gives him several slices of ham that came yesterday from Swayneling Park – a real juicy ham it is, too, Miss, such as I've not seen for many a year."

"Did he actually say he was going on a picnic, Mrs. Hanson?" Rowena persisted.

"I can't rightly recall what he says, Miss Rowena. He just asks me for the sandwiches, stuffs 'em in a knapsack he were a-carrying and was off."

Rowena looked at the Cook with bewildered eyes, then ran upstairs to her father's bed-room.

She knocked and when she entered found that her father had just finished shaving.

He had been called out during the night and was therefore later in rising than usual.

"Sorry to bother you, Papa," she said, "but did Mark say anything to you last night about going on a picnic?"

The Doctor considered for a moment.

"I do not think so, Rowena. When I got home I talked to him until he went to bed about going to Eton. But Hermione was so excited about Florence that I do not think Mark had a chance to say very much."

"Now I think of it he was rather quiet at dinner," Rowena reflected. "I suppose he wants to go to Eton?"

"Of course he does!" Dr. Winsford said. "What boy would not be thrilled at the chance of being sent to the best school in England?"

He finished tying his cravat, and as Rowena helped him into his coat he said wistfully:

"I wish your mother could know what is planned for Hermione and Mark. It is everything she would have wished for them, especially Hermione. She will be very beautiful one day, my dear, like you."

Rowena did not reply and after a moment Dr. Winsford said a little diffidently:

"You do not mind, my dearest, that the Marquis's plans have not included you? I felt it was strange when he did not give you a present after you had nursed him so competently."

"I have no wish, Papa, to be under the Marquis's patronage."

"I would not like you to feel hurt or resentful," Dr. Winsford said.

There was so much tenderness in his tone that Rowena bent forward and kissed him.

"I feel neither of those things, Papa, and if it makes you happy for the Marquis to do so much for the children, then of course I am pleased about it too."

"That is my good girl," Dr. Winsford said, patting her shoulder.

Rowena knew that he was bewildered at the way the Marquis was apparently ignoring her. But it was impossible to explain to him the Marquis's real motives and very underhand ones, for this excess of generosity.

'He is even putting barriers up between my family and me,' she thought, 'so that we can no longer be frank with each other.'

"I must hurry over my breakfast," Dr. Winsford was saying. "I have a lot of work to get through this morning if I am to be at Overton House at half-past-two this afternoon."

"I am glad you have put on your best suit, Papa."

The Doctor smiled.

"Your mother always considered first appearances to be important."

"You look extremely handsome and very smart!" Rowena told him.

The Doctor hurried downstairs. Rowena tidied his bedroom and started to make the bed.

A little later she heard her father leave and knew that he had taken Hermione with him to drop her at Miss Graham's house at the end of the village.

Rowena glanced at the clock and saw it was only half-past-nine. She thought again how strange it was that Mark had gone out so early.

He was usually the difficult one to get out of bed, being

wide-awake in the evening and exceedingly drowsy when it was time to get up.

"I hope he is not going to skip his lessons," she murmured to herself. "The Vicar gets angry when he plays truant."

She walked into her father's Study, repressing as she did so the memory of how magnificent the Marquis had looked the day before standing with his back to the fireplace, his dark hair reflected in the mirror behind him.

Then as she went to her father's desk to try to put some semblance of order into the papers scattered all over it, she saw there was a note propped up against the ink-pot.

She only had to read the word 'Papa' on it to know who it was from. Without hesitation she opened it to find that Mark had written:

"Dear Papa,

I do not wish to go to school. I want to be with horses, so I am going away to earn my living.

Do not worry about me. I have taken half a sovereign from Rowena's housekeeping money and will pay it back as soon as possible.

With love to everybody,
Your affectionate son,

Mark."

Rowena read it through at first quickly, then more slowly. Her lips tightened before she said aloud:

"This is the Marquis's doing . . this is all *his* fault!"

CHAPTER FIVE

"I took the liberty while you were away, My Lord, of ordering a number of new paints and gold and silver leaf that Mr. Gaynor required for his work."

"Quite right, Ashburn," the Marquis replied. "I hope you ordered in large quantities as I have some further work for Mr. Gaynor to begin immediately."

"I will see there is enough, My Lord."

The Marquis signed some papers lying on his desk and handed them to his secretary.

"This letter," he said, "can wait .."

He was interrupted as the door opened.

"Excuse me, M'Lord," the Butler said, "but there is a lady to see you – a Miss Winsford. She says it is urgent."

For a moment the Marquis was still. Then he said:

"Show her in, Newman."

"Very good, M'Lord."

The Butler withdrew and Mr. Ashburn moved towards the door.

Before he got there it opened again and the Butler announced:

"Miss Rowena Winsford, M'Lord!" and Rowena came into the room.

She was looking very pale and her bonnet, though plain and cheap, did not disguise the sun-tints of her hair or the translucence of her blue eyes.

The Marquis rose to his feet, Mr. Ashburn bowed and withdrew as Rowena walked towards the desk.

As the door shut behind his secretary the Marquis asked quietly:

"What has happened?"

"You may well ask," Rowena replied in a low voice. "This is your doing!"

She held out Mark's letter towards him as she spoke and he took it from her, well aware she would not have come to Swayneling Park unless something very untoward had happened.

The Marquis read the note, then he said:

"I am sorry this has occurred. I should have talked to Mark myself. I should have anticipated that he might feel apprehensive at being removed from the environment with which he is familiar and sent away to a strange place."

"I do not believe that would have troubled him if he had not become obsessed with your horses," Rowena said bitterly. "I told you that you were upsetting the whole household, and this is the only one of the disasters which will be the direct result of your interference."

"Suppose we sit down and discuss it?" the Marquis suggested.

"There is nothing to discuss," Rowena replied. "I am here because I wish to speak with your grooms and find out what they have said to Mark, what stories they have told him. He obviously has some idea in his mind as to where he could go to work in someone's stables."

Just for a moment she paused. Then she said in a quieter tone:

"I do not imagine that he would come here."

"I agree that is most unlikely," the Marquis said, "but we will find out."

He crossed the room to where beside the magnificent chimney piece there was a bell-pull.

He tugged at it and almost immediately the door opened and a flunkey in the Swayneling livery with crested buttons stood waiting his command.

"Tell Sam to come here immediately!" the Marquis ordered.

"Very good, M'Lord."

The door shut again, and now the Marquis with a smile which many women had found beguiling said:

"Will you not sit down, Rowena, and may I offer you a glass of wine? Or perhaps you would prefer some chocolate."

"I want nothing, thank you," Rowena answered, "except information about Mark."

She did not look at the Marquis as she spoke, but his eyes were on her face as he said:

"I can only tell you how sorry I am about this. I offered what I thought was the best for your family. You know as well as I do that Mark should go to school."

"My brother and sister are not your responsibility."

"Why not?" the Marquis enquired, "as I intend to make you mine."

"That is something I have no intention of becoming!"

Rowena's eyes were stormy as she went on:

"I know you think you have been very clever, My Lord, in earning the gratitude of my father and making Hermione almost hysterical at the idea of going to Florence. But as far as I am concerned it has only made me hate you more than I was hating you already!"

"You really believe that is true?" the Marquis asked.

There was a note in his voice that made her heart beat even more violently than it had been doing ever since her arrival.

As she had driven up the drive in the chaise with young Lawson, who was the only person she could think of who would bring her quickly to Swayneling Park, she had been overcome by the magnificence of the Marquis's house.

She had expected it to be impressive, but not so beautiful.

It was in fact one of the finest buildings not only in the County but in England.

It had been built in the reign of Elizabeth I by one of her most favoured Statesmen, and the Swaynes had managed all through the centuries to hold positions of power without losing either their heads or their possessions under the succession of different Monarchs adhering to different religions.

From Protestant Elizabeth, through the stormy times of the Stuarts and Commonwealth they not only survived but flourished.

Swayneling Park was a monument not only to the brilliance of their minds but also to the manner in which their marriages had brought them great fortunes and increased estates.

"Nice-looking building, isn't it?" Edward Lawson asked with a side-long glance at Rowena.

She was well aware that during the time it had taken for his horses to bring her here he had been attempting to flirt with her, but she had been too agitated and tense even to be amused by his overtures.

His description, Rowena thought, was hopelessly inadequate, and she could not but feel that the building was a fitting frame and background for the magnificence of the Marquis.

It was just the sort of house she would have expected him to have.

When she entered the marble hall embellished with Greek statues, and was taken along a passage hung with priceless pictures and decorated with fine examples of French furniture, she had, despite herself, felt definitely overawed.

But when she saw the Marquis, even the huge and splendid room in which he was standing sank into insignificance and she was conscious only of him.

Now as he drew a little nearer to her she steeled herself to withstand the way in which he seemed to compel her to a tingling awareness of himself.

She thought he was looking more handsome and even more striking than he had yesterday.

Then she told herself that she was behaving like a rabbit mesmerised by a stoat and that whatever he said or did she hated and despised him for his behaviour towards her.

"Did you think of me last night?" the Marquis asked in a low voice.

"Certainly not!" Rowena declared.

But because she was bad at lying the colour rose in her face and the Marquis laughed softly.

"Could either of us think of anything but each other?" he asked. "You are fighting me, but you know as well as I do, Rowena, that it is a losing battle. We were destined for each other since the beginning of time."

"That is not true," Rowena managed to retort, hoping that her voice sounded positive.

Yet she was vividly aware of an aching sensation within her which made her long to move towards the Marquis and hide her face against his shoulder.

"It was destiny that we should meet," the Marquis went on, "and although I expected to call on you this afternoon, it is destiny that you have come to me now asking for my help."

"It is nothing of the sort!" Rowena managed to say sharply. "What is happening at this moment, My Lord, is, as I have pointed out, entirely the result of your mis-management of my affairs and your interference where it is not wanted."

"Are you telling me that you really do not wish Mark to go to Eton?" the Marquis enquired.

"I would rather he remained uneducated than be beholden to you!"

"If you say that I can only believe that you do not love your brother."

He moved still nearer, and now standing close to her he said softly:

"I shall win in the end, Rowena. Is there any point in continuing to fight me when I hold possession of your heart?"

She thought wildly that that was true, but she was just about to repudiate the suggestion when to her relief the door opened.

"Sam, M'Lord!" the Butler announced and the groom whom Rowena had seen so often in her own home came into the room.

"Good-morning, M'Lord!"

"Good-morning, Sam," the Marquis answered. "Miss Winsford has come here to ask your help."

Sam looked surprised, but after a moment the Marquis went on:

"She wants to know, Sam, what you have said to young Master Mark about working with horses which could make him take it into his head to try to earn his living that way."

Sam's usual smiling face was serious as he said:

"Your Lordship means that the young gentleman's run away?"

"Yes, Sam. He has informed his father that he intends to find work with horses. Now where do you think that could be?"

Sam thought for a moment.

"Oi thinks Master Mark might make for Newmarket, M'Lord."

"You talked to him about the races?"

"Yes, M'Lord, he was very interested and Oi remembers now 'ow Oi told him a large number of stable-boys was required in th' training of th' horses."

The Marquis looked towards Rowena and said:

"That, then, is where Mark will have gone."

"He cannot have got far," Rowena exclaimed. "I should be able to catch up with him."

"I will take you," the Marquis said.

She hesitated a moment before she replied:

"I already have a conveyance."

"With four horses?"

"N .. no."

"Then I think my team will prove quicker. We should be able to overtake Mark on the road to Newmarket before he gets very far."

The Marquis looked towards his groom.

"My Phaeton, Sam, and the new chestnuts!"

"Yes, M'Lord."

Sam hesitated a moment, then he said:

'Oi'm sorry if anythin' Oi said, M'Lord, should have caused any trouble."

"It was not your fault," the Marquis said briefly.

"Thank ye, M'Lord."

The groom went from the room and the Marquis asked Rowena:

"How did you get here?"

"Mr. Lawson from the Livery Stables brought me."

"Of course! Your ardent admirer!" the Marquis remarked sarcastically.

"Papa had already left on his calls, and it may have escaped your notice that we have no other means of transport."

"I will thank the gentleman from the Livery Stables on your behalf," the Marquis said, "and send him about his business!"

He walked across the room as he spoke and Rowena rose to her feet.

"No .. please," she said. "He has been very kind, and .."

The door shut behind the Marquis and she realised there was nothing she could do but allow him to send Edward Lawson away.

She hoped that he would not be anything but polite. At the same time she had to admit to herself that she was glad that she did not have to make the return journey with Mr. Lawson.

He was very persistent in his pursuit and quite impervious to snubs, however frequently they were administered.

At the same time she thought it was typical of the Marquis to be so high-handed leaving her no alternative but to do as he wished.

"All that matters at the moment is to find Mark," Rowena told herself.

Nevertheless, when the Marquis returned a few minutes later to say that he had sent the chaise away and the Phaeton was on its way round from the stables, she could not help feeling a little tremor of excitement because she was to travel with him alone.

There was a groom up behind but he could not overhear what they said, and as they set off down the drive, the Marquis tooling the reins with the expertise which she expected him to show, she thought how many women would be envious of her.

But they had no reason for envy, she told herself bitterly, being sure that any other women whom the Marquis drove would be Ladies of Quality to whom he had a very different attitude.

They drove for a mile or so in silence until the Marquis said:

"You are looking very beautiful this morning, Rowena. Every time I see you I am astonished by your loveliness."

Rowena did not reply, but she clasped her fingers together in her lap over the thin wool rug which covered her gown, and made an effort to control the feelings that the Marquis's compliments always evoked in her.

"I had been planning how I could inveigle you into driving with me," the Marquis went on. "There are so many places I want to show you, so much we might do together. However, as I have said, once again destiny has come to my aid."

"It is not destiny that has brought me here, but Mark! Mark, who has run away because your servants excited him about horses which he will never be able to afford to ride, let alone own."

"Can you be sure of that?" the Marquis asked.

"I am quite sure!" Rowena replied. "Even my father will agree that, while he might accept education for his children, it would be extremely improper for you to supply them with luxuries."

"I see nothing improper about it," the Marquis said. "You know as well as I do, that I am ready to give you the sun, the moon and the stars, and anything else you wish to have."

The words "except for a wedding ring" trembled on Rowena's lips. But thinking it would be ill-bred to make such a remark she remained silent.

"I love you!" the Marquis said, his eyes on his horses ahead. "You have no idea how much I love you. I could not sleep last night for thinking about you."

Rowena would not give him the satisfaction of learning that she had been unable to sleep either.

All she managed to reply coldly was:

"Your idea of love and mine are very different, My Lord, so please let us speak of something else."

"What would you like to talk about?" the Marquis asked. "Shall I tell you that I find the dimples in your cheeks quite irresistible, and I am missing them this morning? Or shall I say that I would give half my fortune at the moment for the privilege of kissing your lips?"

"Stop!" Rowena ordered crossly. "You are not to say such things to me! If you continue to talk to me like this, My Lord, I shall get down and if necessary walk the rest of the way."

"In which case you are unlikely to catch up with your brother, who I am certain walks a great deal faster than you do," the Marquis replied.

This was irrefutable and Rowena lapsed into silence.

They drove on passing the cross-roads which led to Little Powick and now Rowena realised that they were on the road which Mark would have taken, the road which led over the downs to Royston and on to Newmarket.

She remembered that Mark had half a sovereign in his pocket, but she had the idea that he would not expend any of this on taking a Stage-coach.

He was sensible where money was concerned and would be well aware that he might not be fortunate enough to get employment immediately.

She thought however that he might beg a lift on a farm-wagon, and when they had travelled for some miles without a sign of him she was sure this was what had happened.

It seemed as if the Marquis was thinking the same thing, for he said:

"I am imagining what I would do if I were in Mark's place, and I am certain I would look out for a farmer going to market, or perhaps a hay-cart, although that would be slower, trundling in the right direction."

"If we pass a Stage-coach," Rowena replied, "it might be wise to see if Mark is inside."

"He would certainly not be inside," the Marquis replied. "To begin with it is more expensive, and all boys, and most men, prefer to ride on top."

That was true, Rowena thought, and when they passed a Stage-Coach, heavily laden not only with people but with luggage and a variety of coops containing chickens and geese, there were only three men seated outside and no sign of a boy.

Rowena was beginning to think despairingly that perhaps they had made a mistake and Mark was not making for Newmarket.

Her voice trembled as she said:

"Please .. I think we should .. turn back .. perhaps we could try another .. road."

The Marquis looked at her. His eyes rested on her pale cheeks and worried, anxious eyes, before he said:

"We will find him, my darling, that I promise you."

"But .. suppose he is in trouble .. suppose there are men .. who rob .. or hurt him."

The Marquis's lips tightened and he whipped up his horses.

Then as they were driving at what was a tremendous speed down a straight stretch of road Rowena saw ahead a small figure trudging up the next rise.

Instinctively she put out her hand and laid it on the Marquis's arm.

"Is that Mark?" he asked.

"I am .. sure it .. is. Yes .. it is!" Rowena gasped.

She was conscious of such an overwhelming relief that for a

moment she forgot to be on her guard where the Marquis was concerned.

"We have found him!" she cried. "Oh, thank you . . thank you for bringing me to him!"

The Marquis took one hand from the reins to cover hers.

She felt his touch and inevitably it made her quiver. She felt too a sudden weakness which brought tears to her eyes.

She had an irresistible impulse to lay her head against the Marquis's shoulder and tell him how frightened she had been that they would not find Mark and that he was lost to them forever.

Instead with an effort she took her hand away from his arm to sit with her eyes on the small figure ahead of them until the Marquis drew his horses to a halt.

As he did so Mark turned his head.

He was looking rather drawn, Rowena thought, and his boots were very dusty.

"Can we give you a lift?" the Marquis asked. "It is still a long way to where you think you are going."

For a moment Mark seemed quite speechless. Then Rowena leaned out of the Phaeton, her hand outstretched towards him.

"Come home with me, Mark dear," she pleaded. "You know Papa and I cannot lose you."

Just for a moment Mark seemed to hesitate.

Then he looked at the horses and the fineness of them seemed to sweep away the thought of everything else.

"I say, can I drive with you?" he asked. "Is there room?"

"Plenty of room," Rowena answered.

She squeezed herself against the side of the Phaeton so that Mark could climb up and sit between her and the Marquis.

He sat down, and as the Marquis drove on a little way to turn his horses he said somewhat unsteadily:

"I am – sorry if I have put you to any – trouble."

"Did you really think you could disappear without

upsetting your sister?" the Marquis enquired. "I gave you credit for more sense."

There was a curt note in his voice which made Rowena feel uncomfortable.

She put her arm round Mark's shoulders as if to protect him, but he did not relax against her. He merely replied to the Marquis:

"I am sorry, My Lord, I did not think."

"Then you should," the Marquis answered. "If you had waited, I had intended this afternoon when I came to your father's house to talk to you about your riding."

"My – riding?"

"I was going to suggest that for the rest of the holidays I should lend you a horse and a groom, and if your progress is good, as I am sure it will be, that you could come out hunting when you come home at Christmas."

For a moment Mark's breath was taken away. Then he said:

"Hunting! Did you say – hunting, My Lord?"

"That is what I said," the Marquis replied, "but of course you may prefer to be a stable-lad and spend at least a year mucking out stables, or if you are fortunate being allowed to groom the horses."

There was silence, then Mark said:

"I realise I have made a fool of myself, My Lord."

"Another time when you feel rebellious or not quite certain what is the right thing to do, you might talk it over with me," the Marquis suggested. "I am quite experienced in such matters, having been a boy myself at one time."

"I will, My Lord, and thank you very much!" Mark agreed. "Did you really mean that I could ride until I go to school?"

"I meant it," the Marquis replied, "and I have another suggestion to make."

Mark was gazing up at him rapturously, but Rowena was staring straight ahead of her, her lips pressed together.

She realised that after this Mark would worship the

Marquis with adoration which nothing she could say or do would shake.

A horse for the holidays! Hunting at Christmas! How could she compete with that?

"I hate him! I hate him!" she told herself.

And yet it was impossible not to realise that what he was suggesting would open new horizons for Mark and make all the difference to his life.

They drove to Little Powick and Rowena never spoke, while Mark with shining eyes talked excitedly of horses, interspersed with almost a paean of gratitude for what the Marquis had promised him.

When the Phaeton drew up outside the door of their house Mark asked eagerly:

"May I go to their heads, My Lord?"

"If you wish," the Marquis replied.

Mark jumped down from the Phaeton before it came to a standstill to beat Sam to the horses' heads.

As Rowena pulled back the rug which covered her gown, the Marquis said in a low voice:

"Am I forgiven?"

"No!"

"That is ungenerous of you."

"You are merely bribing him, just as you have bribed Hermione and of course Papa."

"I think that is an unpleasant word."

"What you are doing is unpleasant. You are cheating in order to get your own way."

"I have always been told that all is fair in love and war, and this is both, Rowena."

"It is certainly war," she answered, "and as you are pre-pared to use every weapon in your power, I shall do the same."

The Marquis did not answer.

With a swiftness that was surprising in a man who had been so recently injured he climbed down from the Phaeton on his side and before she could step down was waiting to assist her.

It was impossible for her to avoid him, and as he lifted her to the ground he held her close against him.

Despite every resolution, despite telling herself firmly that she was furious with him, she felt her heart turn over and an unmistakable thrill run through her body.

She felt to her annoyance that the Marquis was aware of it, for there was a smile on his lips as he saw her face and swept his hat from his head.

"As I am sure you are feeling inhospitable," he said, "I will not invite myself in."

As he spoke Mark came from the horses' heads to stand beside him and he continued:

"I was going to tell you, Mark, that I have to go to London first thing in the morning."

"You are going away?"

There was no doubt of the dismay in the boy's voice.

"Only for three or four days," the Marquis said reassuringly. "You may not know it but all London is celebrating on August 1st and the Regent wishes to pay a special tribute to the Duke of Wellington. He is giving a huge party at Carlton House at which I must be present."

"You will not stay long?"

"I shall return as soon as possible," the Marquis answered. "Perhaps on the 2nd, but certainly on the 3rd. Then I was going to suggest that you should come to Swayneling Park and we will choose a horse for you to ride until the beginning of September."

"Is that when I start at Eton?" Mark asked.

"Yes," the Marquis answered, "and I intend to tell you a great deal about the school, which will make it seem less strange and frightening when you get there."

"Thank you, My Lord, thank you very much!" Mark answered and added irrepressibly, "You will not forget my horse?"

"I promise you that I will send for you or come and collect you myself the moment I return from London."

The Marquis smiled and said:

"You might spend the time between in catching up with your lessons and getting ahead. It would be a pity for them to interfere with the time you might be riding."

He spoke lightly, but Rowena knew that Mark understood it was an order.

"I promise I will do that," he answered.

As the Marquis was talking to Mark she waited just inside the hall door, feeling it would be rude to move away. At the same time she was aware because of the emotions within her that she would be wise to go.

"Now everything is settled satisfactorily," the Marquis said, "and I hope, Rowena, that you too will be looking forward to my return."

With Mark listening there was nothing she could do but to curtsey.

She would not have given the Marquis her hand but he reached out and took it, and before she could prevent him, he raised it to his lips.

She had taken off her glove while he was talking, and now she felt his mouth against her bare skin.

Involuntarily her fingers tightened on his.

He raised his head and looked into her eyes, his face close to hers.

She knew in that moment they were both very still. Then the Marquis put his hat on his head.

"Good-bye, Mark," he said. "Take care of your sister. She is a very special person."

He climbed back into the Phaeton, Sam released the horses' heads and they started off before the groom had scrambled into the seat beside his master.

Because she did not wish to see him go Rowena went into the house leaving Mark waving from the steps until the horses were out of sight.

Rowena had reached the top of the stairs when Mark hailed her from the hall.

"I say, Rowena, could anything be more marvellous? You do not think he will forget?"

"No, I am certain he will not," Rowena replied dryly.

She moved towards her room, but Mark's voice arrested her again.

"Is Papa angry with me?"

Rowena turned back to lean over the banisters.

"Papa does not know, Mark. I did not tell him. You are to promise me that you will not mention that you went away. It would upset him terribly."

"No, of course I will not mention it," Mark answered. "It was jolly decent of you, Rowena, not to tell him."

"He had left the house and did not see your note. I will tear it up and we will forget that it ever happened. Is that understood?"

Mark nodded.

Then he gave a cry that seemed to echo round the hall.

"Hunting, Rowena! I am going to hunt. Just think of it!"

'It is no use,' Rowena thought, 'the Marquis has captured him completely.'

He had won the battle over Hermione and Mark and, she had to admit, where her father was concerned.

That left only Lotty, who was too young to matter, and herself.

"He shall not win!" Rowena said aloud as she reached her bed-room. "If he is prepared to use any means and any weapons to get his own way, then I must use the only one I have left."

* * * * *

Rowena, travelling to London by Stage-coach, was wondering whether the Marquis's superlative horses drawing his big-wheeled Phaeton which could travel four times as quickly would pass them on the road.

She thought however as she had left so early in the morning that it was unlikely.

She was hoping as she sat squeezed between a farmer's fat wife and an even stouter gentleman who was travelling as a representative of a wine firm, that her father would not be worried when he read the letter she had left for him.

For the first time since she could remember Rowena had lied.

She had told him that she was journeying to London at the Marquis's suggestion to see about clothes for Hermione to take with her to Florence. She thought she might stay one night, if not two, and felt sure that he and the children could manage without her.

Her father would be surprised. At the same time Rowena thought that in his usual trustful manner he would not suspect that she was doing anything but what she said she intended to do.

'If I fail,' she told herself, 'then I can come back this evening.'

She was certain that any searching questions there might be would come from Hermione and not her father.

The Stage-coach rumbled along the country roads, throwing up a great deal of dust until the roads improved, there were more houses and they had reached the outskirts of London.

It was then Rowena wished she had taken a seat on top of the coach, knowing she would not have been so hot and uncomfortable and would have been able to get a better view as they entered the city.

But she had been afraid that the Marquis might notice her as he sped past, and that was the one thing she was determined must not happen under any circumstances.

It was unlikely, and yet it was a possibility, and she was resolved that in this venture, if in nothing else, she could take no risks.

It was quite by chance that yesterday evening she had turned almost unconsciously to the Social Column in the *Morning Post* to see if there was anything written about the celebrations for the Duke of Wellington to which the Marquis had referred.

She knew that the Prince Regent's party would be written

up after the event, but she told herself that she was not concerned with the social aspect. It was the tributes the ordinary people were paying to the hero of Waterloo which were interesting.

To her surprise Rowena found that a most elaborate gala was being arranged in the London Parks to celebrate the anniversary of the Battle of the Nile and the centenary of the accession to the English throne of the House of Hanover.

In St. James's Park, a Chinese Pagoda was being erected and a picturesque yellow bridge ornamented with a bright blue roof.

In Green Park there was an embattled Gothic castle over a hundred feet square, in Hyde Park booths, stalls, arcades, kiosks, swings and roundabouts.

Lanterns were to line Birdcage Walk and the Mall, and it was reported that five hundred men had been at work for a month to produce the 'most brilliant fireworks ever seen in the country'.

The *Morning Post* promised a spectacle of 'unparalleled splendour', but Rowena wondered what all this had to do with the Iron Duke.

It was hard after so many years of war to realise that peace had come at last and the privations from which they had all suffered would gradually disappear.

'Perhaps food will be cheaper,' Rowena told herself hopefully.

She knew that already the farmers were apprehensive that without a war they would no longer be so much in demand.

'I expect on the whole it will make very little difference to us,' Rowena thought.

She could understand that the Marquis, who she had learnt while he was staying in their house, had served under Wellington for five years, must be present when his Commander was the Guest of Honour at Carlton House.

But while there was no mention of the Marquis or of the Prince's party in the *Social Gazette*, there was a paragraph which Rowena read several times before she put down the newspapers to stand thinking reflectively in her father's Study.

This, she told herself, was the weapon she had been seeking, a weapon with which she could fight the Marquis and defeat him once and for all.

The question was, dare she use it?

Then she told herself she had nothing to lose. If she was rebuffed, ignored or insulted, no-one would know but herself. She would never in any circumstances let her father learn of what he personally would think of as a betrayal.

The thought of her father made Rowena hesitate. But she told herself that the vital thing was to make the Marquis understand once and for all that she would not do what he asked of her.

"Oh, Mama, help me!" she cried, raising her eyes to where hanging over her father's desk there was a portrait of her mother painted soon after they had been married.

Rowena had inherited her mother's hair and eyes, her heart-shaped face and sweet expression. Yet at nineteen she felt she was immeasurably older in so many ways than her mother had ever been.

She had no longer the trusting faith with which she met the world before she encountered the Marquis. He had disillusioned her and destroyed her ideals.

'I loved him,' she thought, 'I loved him wholeheartedly, and it seemed when he kissed me as if our love was a part of God.'

But it had been nothing of the sort. It had merely been a temptation of the devil, and once again Rowena told herself that she hated him and everything he stood for.

It was then that she made up her mind.

"I will go to London," she said aloud.

The Stage-coach rumbled into the yard of the Two Headed Swan at Islington and the passengers alighted.

Although she felt shocked at the amount of money she was spending Rowena realised that from there she would have to take a hackney carriage to take her to Curzon Street.

She had no idea of how otherwise she could get there, and moreover to waste time would mean there would be no chance of her returning home that evening.

The driver of the hackney carriage knew Dunvegan House to which she asked to be taken, and only when it stopped outside a tall, gloomy mansion did Rowena realise that her hands were trembling and her mouth felt dry.

Nevertheless having paid off the driver she walked firmly up the steps and raised the knocker on the door.

It was some seconds before she heard footsteps and the door was opened by a very old servant wearing a livery in which he appeared to have shrunk so that it hung loosely from his shoulders.

If he appeared decrepit, the two footmen behind him with powdered wigs were tall and upstanding, and Rowena saw that the inside of the hall while cluttered with heavy, ponderous furniture, was impressive.

"I wish to speak with the Earl of Dunvegan."

"Is His Lordship expecting you?" the old Butler asked in a quivering voice.

"No," Rowena admitted. "But will you please tell His Lordship that his grand-daughter desires to speak with him."

She saw the surprise in the old man's eyes. Then he shuffled across the hall to open a door.

"Will you wait in here, Miss?" he asked.

The room was decorated with tasselled curtains of dark red velvet which precluded most of the light, and huge pieces of mahogany furniture.

Rowena hardly looked around her.

She was waiting breathlessly for the Butler's return.

It seemed to her that she waited a long time: it might have been months rather than minutes.

Then there were the shuffling footsteps on the uncarpeted marble floor and the door opened.

"Will you come this way, Miss?"

He could not move quickly and Rowena could not help wishing that one of the footmen had escorted her.

Moving at a snail's pace they came to two impressive double doors which the Butler flung open.

It was a big room looking out to the back of the house, and sitting stiffly upright beside the empty hearth was an elderly man.

Rowena had only to look at him to know that he was exactly what she had expected her mother's father would look like.

An aristocrat with his clear-cut Roman nose, shrewd perceptive eyes under heavy eye-brows, a mouth and chin which bespoke an obstinacy and a determination equalled only, she thought, by that of the Marquis.

He seemed to be a long way away as Rowena walked towards him.

Only when she reached the hearth-rug did she stop to look at him, her eyes very wide and anxious in her small face.

"You are my grand-daughter?"

The voice was sharp and there was nothing elderly about it.

Rowena curtsied.

"I am Rowena Winsford."

"You are very like your mother."

"Yes , but she was very beautiful."

"Has she sent you to me?"

"She is dead. She died two years ago."

"Dead!"

There was a note in the old man's voice which told her this was a shock, something he had not expected.

"She died soon after Christmas because it was so cold. She had pneumonia, and we could not afford fuel to keep the house warm."

Rowena thought she saw his lips tighten, but she was not certain.

She had the feeling that he was too self-controlled to reveal an emotion of any sort.

"Why have you come to see me?"

"I need your help."

"Can your father not give you that?"

"I am not asking for financial help," Rowena said quickly, "it is too late for that. It would have helped Mama, but you know she would not have approached you."

There was silence for a moment. Then the Earl of Dunvegan said:

"You had better sit down and explain yourself."

This was a considerable concession, as Rowena was aware. She saw there was a chair near the one in which he was sitting and she sat down gratefully, feeling her legs were weak as if she had suffered from a long illness.

"Where have you come from?"

"We live in the country, not far from Hatfield."

"And you knew I was in London?"

"I saw it in the *Morning Post*."

"But I live in Scotland as perhaps you are aware."

"Mama told me about you shortly before she died. I had no idea until then who she was before she married, or that she had run away with Papa."

"She doubtless told you that when she left my house she ceased to be my daughter?"

"Yes, she told me that is what you said; but she loved Papa and she was very, very happy with him."

There was a moment's silence. Then, as if he could not control his curiosity, the Earl asked:

"And you are her only child?"

"No, there is Hermione who is sixteen, Mark who is twelve, and Lotty who is eight."

"I hope your father can afford them."

"We manage."

"Then why do you need my help?"

"That is what I want to tell you," Rowena said. "I want to make it very clear that I am not begging. Mama had the same pride that you had, and she said that I had your obstinacy."

Just for a moment there was a faint smile on the Earl's lips as he said:

"Are you obstinate?"

"I think so, certainly with regard to one thing. And that is why I am here."

"And what is that?"

Rowena hesitated for a moment, then she said:

"It concerns the Marquis of Swayne."

"I know him. What has he to do with you?"

"He wants me to become his mistress!"

"His mistress? What the devil is your father doing about it?"

There was no doubt that Rowena had startled the old man, as she had intended.

"Papa knows nothing about it. The Marquis had an accident and was brought to our house. I nursed him."

"And fell in love with him, I suppose?"

Rowena paused for a moment.

"Yes .. I fell in love with him, and I thought he was in love with me."

"So he offered you his – protection."

There was no doubt of the sneer behind the words.

"I thought, because he said he loved me, that he wished to marry me," Rowena said simply.

There was silence. Then the Earl of Dunvegan said:

"He was not prepared to make a Doctor's daughter his wife, I presume."

"No, and ever since I refused him, he will not leave us alone."

Speaking quickly Rowena told her grandfather what the Marquis was doing.

"Papa thinks he is being generous because he saved his life," she said. "How can I tell him that he is simply trying to blackmail me into agreeing to what he wants?"

"You would not consider accepting such a proposal?"

"Do you think Mama would have countenanced it? She was your daughter. You know how she would never do anything to hurt anyone. She believed in God and everything that was right and good."

There was a little throb in Rowena's voice. Then as her grandfather did not speak she said:

"I have a plan by which I believe I could get rid of the Marquis. But I cannot do so except with your help."

"What are you suggesting?" her grandfather asked.

Hesitatingly and a little shyly Rowena told him.

He listened to her and when she had finished he said:

"And you think that he will then ask you to marry him?"

Rowena stiffened.

"Do you think I would marry him in those circumstances?" she asked. "Not if he was the last man in the world! Never! Never!"

She drew in her breath. Then, as if she was afraid her grandfather would not believe her, she said:

"I hate him! I hate him for his behaviour towards me, for what he suggested, which I know is wrong and wicked!"

Her voice seemed to ring out round the dark room. Then as the Earl still did not speak, Rowena moved from the chair to kneel beside him.

"Please help me, Grandfather," she said. "There is no-one else I can ask. I am afraid of him .. afraid that he will get the family into his clutches .. and then I shall be unable to .. go on .. defying him."

She looked up at her grandfather as she spoke and felt for one moment that she had failed and he was going to refuse.

Then slowly, very slowly, the hard line of his mouth twisted into a smile.

"I think," the Earl said as if he chose every word with care, "that the Marquis of Swayne needs a sharp lesson!"

CHAPTER SIX

The Regent in his Field Marshal's full-dress, wearing his English, Russian, Prussian and French Orders, looked extremely impressive.

There was nothing he enjoyed more than the congenial task of arranging a fête at Carlton House, and this one, which he intended as a personal tribute to the Duke of Wellington, was very dear to his heart.

The first act of his 'unrestricted Regency' had been to sign the Warrant for a pension for the hero of Waterloo, and it was with the Duke in mind that the Regent had designed the whole fête.

A special polygonal building had been put up in the garden.

It was a solid structure, one hundred and twenty feet in diameter, built of brick and with a leaded roof; but the interior was designed to give the impression of summer light, airiness and festivity.

This effect had been achieved by painting the umbrella-shaped ceiling to resemble muslin and by decorating it with gilt cords, by fixing looking-glass to the walls and hanging them with muslin draperies.

The whole effect, enhanced by the sparkling illumination of twelve chandeliers, was delightful.

Huge banks of artificial flowers were arranged on the floor in the shape of a temple behind whose walls of petals and foliage were concealed two bands.

A covered promenade decorated with draperies of rose-coloured cords led to a Corinthian Temple where the guests were able to admire a marble bust of the great Duke of Turnerelli placed on a column in front of a large mirror.

This was engraved with a star and the letter 'W'.

In the garden there were supper tents and refreshment rooms hung with white and rose curtains and with regimental colours printed on silk.

"What do you think of it, Swayne?" the Regent asked the Marquis.

"It does you credit, Sire," the Marquis replied and the Regent beamed at him.

His Royal Highness had also concerned himself with the preparation of the galas in the London Parks.

Only *The Times*, in contrast to the eulogies written in the other newspapers, had struck a gloomy note in remarking that 'the public would first gape at the mummery, then laugh at the authors of it and lastly grumble at the expense'.

It seemed on the morning of August 1st that *The Times*'s peevish prophecies of disaster were about to be fulfilled when there was a heavy fall of rain. But between ten o'clock and eleven the sun came out and the celebrations began.

The Marquis from his house in Park Lane had heard the noise and the rockets shooting in the sky each one containing 'a world of smaller rockets'.

There were also echoes from the Regatta on the Serpentine where a splendid 'naumachia' representing the Battle of the Nile ended with the French fleet being destroyed by fireships.

But he was kept far too busy by the Regent at Carlton House to have time to see what was happening elsewhere.

As a close friend both of his Royal Highness and of the Duke himself, the Marquis found himself making decisions on protocol, on the seating at the supper-tables, and on a thousand other matters.

These completely occupied his attention until the first of the two thousand guests invited to Carlton House began to arrive at nine o'clock.

They were received at the Grand Entrance by Equerries

who conducted them to the various rooms, tents and corridors on the garden front.

The Regent received those he knew well, and from the first moment there was a queue waiting to shake the hand of the Duke himself.

The Regent prided himself on his good memory but that did not prevent him from continually asking the Marquis the names of those advancing towards him and hoping for recognition.

"Who is that lady?" he enquired now.

The Marquis, looking up from the plans of the supper tables that he held in his hand, saw an extremely beautiful woman laden with diamonds and recognised her as an old flirt.

"Lady Warburton, Sire."

"Of course! Of course!" the Regent said.

He held out his hand as Lady Warburton curtsied and greeted her effusively which made her smile at him beguilingly.

"Damned pretty woman!" he remarked to the Marquis as she moved away. "See she is at my table at supper."

The Marquis sighed.

He had already changed the supper plan a dozen times and he wondered now who he could remove to another table without giving offence.

"And who is this?" the Regent asked.

The Marquis raised his head and saw coming into the room a magnificent figure in full Highland dress. From the bunch of lace under his proudly held chin to the swing of his silver ornamented sporran it was easy to recognise that here was a Chieftain of great importance.

For a moment the Marquis hesitated, then said with the air of a conjuror bringing a rabbit out of a hat:

"I have it! The Earl of Dunvegan, Sire."

"Of course, I recognised him instantly!"

The Earl bowed his head and the Regent held out his hand.

"I could not anticipate that we would be honoured by

123

your presence, My Lord," he said, "when I know that you so seldom come South."

"I consider it a privilege to be present on such an occasion," the Earl replied.

"Then I must tell you how very welcome you are," the Regent responded.

"You are very gracious," the Earl answered. "May I, Sire, present my grand-daughter who has not previously been to London?"

"Of course! Of course!"

Rowena curtsied and the Regent said:

"She is very pretty, My Lord, very pretty indeed! You must be proud of her."

"I am!" the Earl replied.

The Regent was holding Rowena's hand for longer than was necessary.

"What is your name, my dear?" he enquired, looking down at her face with that swimmy look in his eyes which every pretty woman evoked almost automatically.

"Rowena, Sire."

"Then you will certainly be one of the most beautiful women at my fête this evening."

As Rowena spoke the Marquis had raised his head.

For a moment his glance was casual because the name rang a bell. Then as he saw who was speaking to the Regent the expression of astonishment on his face was very obvious.

"Good-evening, Swayne!"

The Earl was speaking to him and it was with an effort that the Marquis managed to reply:

"Good-evening, My Lord. It is a long time since we met."

"It is indeed. You came with your father, if I remember rightly, to stay at my Castle, perhaps seven years ago?"

"I think it was eight, to be precise, My Lord."

"Eight then – we have all grown older in the intervening time."

"That is true, My Lord."

"She is enchanting! Quite enchanting!" the Regent was

exclaiming. "Swayne, make quite certain that the Earl of Dunvegan and his grand-daughter Rowena are at my table for supper."

'Very good, Sire."

'I believe you know my grand-daughter," the Earl remarked to the Marquis.

"We have met, My Lord."

Rowena's eyes met those of the Marquis.

As he looked at her he could hardly believe that he was not dreaming.

She certainly appeared very different from when he had last seen her.

Her gown of white gauze was in the latest fashion, her fair hair was arranged in a style that he was aware had only just reached London from the Continent.

Round her neck there was a collet of pure blue-white diamonds which he supposed was part of the Dunvegan collection.

He felt as if his brain was not functioning, and it was impossible to find anything to say to her or even indeed to acknowledge the graceful curtsey she had made him when her grandfather introduced them.

"We shall doubtless see you again at supper, My Lord," the Earl remarked.

Then taking Rowena by the arm he drew her out through the open windows into the garden.

There was so much to see, not only on the walls of the covered walk which, decorated in green calico was coloured with transparencies representing such appropriate subjects as 'Military Glory' and the 'Over-throw of Tyranny by the Allied Powers', but also inside the house.

Rowena had always longed to see the Chinese Room and the Blue Drawing-Room with its priceless collection of pictures and exquisite miniatures.

But even while her grandfather showed her the treasures of the Regent's collection she found it hard not to think all the time of the Marquis.

She had surprised him, in fact astounded him which was what she had set out to do.

She knew too, that the unimportant Doctor's daughter had struck him with a blow which was all the more powerful because it encroached on his special and personal hobby.

No-one could deny that the Dunvegan family tree not only equalled that of the Swaynes but, having played an integral part in the whole history of Scotland might be also said to exceed them.

When Rowena had first learnt from her mother of the Earl's fury at his only daughter wishing to marry an obscure country Doctor, she had felt a bitter resentment against her grandfather's snobbery.

This had later transferred itself to a positive and personal dislike of the Marquis's preoccupation with Genealogy.

It seemed incredible that her grandfather, although he might be the Premier Earl of Scotland, had not appreciated her father's upright and noble character and had not cared that he had made her mother, as she had said so often, 'the happiest woman in the world'.

The fact that the marriage had been forbidden and her mother had rebelled to the point of running away, had seemed to Rowena to make her grandfather into a tyrant with whom she had no wish ever to communicate.

"I am telling you this as an absolute secret, Rowena," her mother had said when she confided in her. "You must never speak of it to your father, because it upsets him.

"He worries so much that I gave up my social life and the comforts I had as a girl to live with him in obscurity, and to some extent poverty; but it has never mattered in the least to me."

Her face had lit up with a smile of almost perfect happiness as she added:

"No man in the world could be as wonderful as your father. As I have told you before, Rowena, he was my destiny."

"But Mama, if you had called yourself by your proper name, if you had let people know you were Lady Elizabeth

Winsford, perhaps it would have helped Papa to obtain more important and wealthy patients."

"That would have hurt your father's pride," Rowena's mother had answered quickly. "My father had accused him of being unable to keep me so he was determined to do without any help from a family which had cast me out and told me that I no longer belonged to them."

"That must have been very hurtful, Mama," Rowena said sympathetically.

"It only hurt me because they disparaged and tried to belittle your father. But our love was greater than rank or money and like Ruth, my people became his people, my country – his country."

Rowena had flung her arms around her mother and kissed her.

"I think it was very brave and wonderful of you, Mama, to run away. I do not believe I would ever be brave enough in the same circumstances."

"I think you would be," her mother answered. "Sometimes you are very like your grandfather. You have his obstinacy, his same tenacity of purpose."

That, Rowena told herself now, was why she had sought out her grandfather and enlisted his help in a battle which to her was more important at the moment even than her loyalty to her father.

'Now the Marquis will be ashamed of his behaviour towards me,' she thought.

She wished at the same time that her triumph did not leave an ache in her heart from the thought that now, even if he did ask her to marry him, she could never accept.

In spite of all the exciting things there were to see and the superlative supper she enjoyed at the Regent's table amongst a glittering and distinguished company, Rowena found it hard not to keep looking for the Marquis.

She saw him at supper, but he was sitting far away from her at almost the other end of the table.

She felt a little pang of jealousy because on either side of him were two of the most attractive and beautiful women she had ever seen, both resplendently bejewelled.

The Marquis was obviously well satisfied with his supper partners and as they leant towards him their bare shoulders frequently touched his close-fitting evening-coat embellished with numerous decorations.

'Those are the sort of women he prefers,' Rowena thought, 'and what have they in common with a Doctor's daughter?'

The supper came to an end, but there was no question of anyone leaving.

The Queen, who had entertained three hundred guests to a banquet at Buckingham House, arrived late, and did not sit down to supper until two o'clock.

The people who had come with her were all talking of the disaster in Green Park when the Pagoda with its Japanese lanterns and gas-jets spluttering on its blue roof, had burst into flames.

It had collapsed into the waters of the lake, killing a lamplighter and injuring five other workmen, but this was accepted by the crowd as yet another brilliantly contrived spectacle.

The Earl of Dunvegan had been greeted effusively by the Duke of Wellington and had found a number of friends amongst the Commanders of the Scottish Regiments.

There was so much conversation about Scotland that Rowena wandered away by herself to admire the artificial streams trickling through the gardens and the exquisite arrangements of flowers.

She was staring at some which were unfamiliar and she thought must have been brought from abroad, when a deep voice behind her asked:

"Why did you not tell me?"

She felt her heart leap. At the same time she had enough control over herself not to turn around.

She did not answer and after a moment the Marquis asked:

"How could I have guessed that the Earl of Dunvegan was your grandfather?"

"He disowned my mother on her marriage," Rowena replied, "and I had no desire to make his acquaintance until I realised that I might find him a protector."

There was no need for her to elaborate what she meant. She was quite certain the Marquis would take her meaning.

"Have you told your family that you are here?"

This was the weak point in her whole scheme, and it was typical, she thought bitterly, that he should at once put his finger on it.

"No," she replied, "and I can only ask you not to hurt my father by telling him."

She paused, then turning round she said:

"It is none of your business, as you well know! And now I hope, My Lord, that you will realise that I am serious in asking you to leave me alone and not to bother me as you have done in the past."

"Do you mean that?" the Marquis enquired.

Rowena forced herself to look up at him. His face was very clear in the light of the Japanese lantern which hung from the branches of an adjacent tree.

He did not wait for a reply but after a moment said:

"You look very lovely! I have never before seen you looking fashionable and wearing diamonds. I only wish they were mine that encircled your neck."

"You realise now that I have asked my grandfather to protect me."

"And you think he can manage to do that?"

"I think you will consider that he speaks to you as an equal when he commands you to leave me alone."

The Marquis laughed softly.

"Your eyes are flashing, which you know I find extremely alluring," he said. "Do you really believe, Rowena, that I am so faint-hearted that I accept defeat so easily? That I am afraid of the claymores of the Scots?"

There was amused scorn in the Marquis's voice as he went on:

"Where you are concerned I will never acknowledge defeat. I will go on fighting for you until you surrender as your heart longs to, however much your brain may tell you otherwise."

"I hate you!" Rowena exclaimed.

"On the contrary," the Marquis answered, "you love me, my darling, just as I love you. We belong to each other."

'You are quite wrong, and I refuse to listen to you."

Some people passed by near them, and knowing the Marquis dare not make a scene Rowena turned and walked away from him back to her grandfather's side.

They did not leave the party until what seemed to her to be very late, but as they were driving towards Curzon Street in the Earl's carriage she said:

"I would like you, Grandfather, to speak to the Marquis and tell him to leave me alone."

"I saw him talking to you," the Earl answered. "Has he now, knowing you are my grand-daughter, proposed marriage?"

"He merely said he would go on fighting for me," Rowena said. "I do not think that even he would sink so low as to change so quickly simply because he realises I am not so common as he thought me to be."

"If I were a younger man, I would doubtless challenge him to a duel," the Earl remarked. "But as it is, I will tell him in no uncertain terms what I think of his behaviour."

"Please do, Grandfather! Perhaps he will call on me to-morrow before I leave London."

The Earl was silent for a moment. Then he said:

"You intend to return home?"

"Yes, Grandfather. I would not wish the family to know where I have been or why I had to come to London. There would be too many explanations to make."

"I can understand that," the Earl replied, "at the same time I shall be sorry to lose you."

This was a concession that she had not expected to hear from him, and Rowena impulsively slipped her hand into his.

"I think Mama would have been glad that we met each other," she said. "Perhaps one day I could see you again."

"I would like to take you north with me," the Earl said gruffly. "I was proud of you to-night, my dear. Though my son has three children, you are my eldest grand-daughter."

"I am glad about that," Rowena said, "and I would love to meet my cousins. But you must realise it is impossible. Papa would be so hurt .. which is why I must never let him know that I came to you for help."

The Earl held her hand and after a moment Rowena said:

"Hermione is going to be very beautiful, and Lotty is like Mama. Perhaps one day you could receive them."

"We must think about it," the Earl said. "Perhaps when you are married to Swayne you will come and stay with me."

Rowena jumped as if she had been stabbed.

"Marry the Marquis?" she exclaimed. "You know, Grandfather, that is the one thing I am determined not to do!"

"But you love him?"

There was silence in the carriage. Then after a moment Rowena admitted:

"Yes, I love him, but I also despise him. We could never find happiness together when all the time I was aware that he would never have married me except that I have your blood in my veins."

There was so much unhappiness in her voice that the Earl's fingers tightened on hers before he said:

"You do not think you are asking too much? Blood is thicker than water, my dear, and all of us who belong to the great families have a deep pride in our history and in our antecedents."

She knew he was speaking of his reason for not accepting her father when he wished to marry her mother. After a moment Rowena answered:

"Mama was ideally happy, despite knowing that Papa came from very ordinary stock. If the Marquis had been prepared to marry me when he thought I was just 'Miss Winsford', I know we too would have been happy together. But now there is an insurmountable barrier between us which nothing he can say or do could ever bridge."

"It is a pity," the Earl said. "He may be rather puffed up with his own conceit, but the Duke was telling me to-night that he was an excellent soldier and leader of men."

"You spoke about him to the Duke?"

"I was interested to learn His Grace's reaction," the Earl remarked.

Rowena was sure that the Duke had been right. The Marquis would be a good soldier. He would be reliable and also a determined commander who would never accept defeat.

He would win against all odds, she thought, except where she was concerned.

As she had told her grandfather, there was now an insurmountable barrier between them.

She knew that, even if the Marquis went down on his knees and begged her to be his wife, she could never feel about him what she had felt when he first kissed her and she knew there was for her nothing and nobody in the world but him.

Alone in her bed-room she sat at the mirror looking at her reflection and thinking this was the last time she would see herself looking so fashionable, and that diamonds would never again flash round her throat.

The diamonds were of course part of the Dunvegan Collection. Before they had set out for Carlton House the Earl had taken a number of boxes from the safe and opened them for Rowena's inspection.

The jewels, although many of them were heavily set, were magnificent. There were necklaces in emeralds, sapphires and amethysts.

The diamond collet was the simplest, even though the

large blue-white stones were doubtless more valuable than some of the others. Rowena had asked if she could wear it and her grandfather had clasped it round her neck.

The gown she wore had been brought hastily to the house with several others from an expensive Court Dressmaker in Bond Street.

Fortunately they required little alteration, and the one she chose to go to Carlton House was in fact the most beautiful gown she had ever seen.

"How can I thank you, Grandfather?" she had asked when she put it on to show him.

"You make me think of your mother," he replied simply.

She knew that was all the thanks he required and the reason why he was taking her with him, as she had asked, to Carlton House.

When she daringly kissed him good-night before she went upstairs to bed, she had thought that he was surprised, but at the same time pleased.

"Thank you, Grandfather," she said. "It was a great adventure to be with you and meet not only the Regent but all those other interesting people. I shall never forget how kind you have been!"

"I shall remember it too," the Earl conceded.

Rowena looked at him for a moment. Then she asked the question that was uppermost in her mind.

"Grandfather, is the pride which you and the Marquis feel in your families worth the heart-ache and unhappiness that it causes when it comes into conflict with love?"

The old man looked at her from under his bushy eyebrows. Then he replied:

"Our ancestors have fought and died for that pride all down the centuries. It is ingrained in us. It is something that is inescapable. If we denied it, we would feel we were renegades and traitors."

He spoke with a sincerity that was very impressive.

Rowena gave a little sigh.

"I understand," she said, "at least .. I think I do. I

suppose I am one of the hundreds, perhaps thousands of people who must suffer under that pride."

"Yet for many others," the Earl answered, "it has been the dominant influence in their lives and has brought them satisfaction and at times a glory that was greater than any personal gratification could ever bring."

There was a finality about the way he spoke which told Rowena there could be no more argument about it.

As she went up to bed she lay thinking over his words, realising he spoke not only for himself but also for the Marquis and perhaps all the other noble families who dedicated themselves to their duty.

And yet, Rowena longed to argue, there were many families whose members had married those considered to be parvenus and of inferior blood.

But the answer was obvious: they had had something to offer that was advantageous for the whole family and not just for one member of it, – a great fortune, acres of land, magnificent buildings or streets and squares in London whose rents swelled the family exchequer.

"And I have nothing!" Rowena said wistfully, "except a pretty face, and that is not enough."

The memory of how the Marquis had tried to explain that he could not offer her marriage haunted her as it had done night after night ever since it happened.

She could see him standing by the window as he spoke, choosing his words with care. She could hear his voice saying:

"I should have explained to you before that marriage and love in the world in which I live are two very different things."

Then, as the meaning of what he was saying had seemed like a knife-thrust in her heart, he had gone on:

"It is a question of noble blood being matched by noble blood, of putting the family first and being true to one's inheritance."

That was what he truly believed and what her grandfather had believed when he had turned her father away from the house and forbidden a marriage between him and her mother.

Rowena knew that nothing she could say or do would alter their feelings or dissuade them from sacrificing their emotions to what they believed was a sacred trust.

She only hoped as she lay in the darkness that the Marquis was suffering as she was, knowing that when he had refused to marry her he had destroyed their only chance of happiness.

'If he had been more perceptive,' Rowena told herself, 'if he had been in the least fey, he would have known I was not the commoner I appeared to be, but that I, too, had blue blood in my veins . . as blue as his.'

Then she told herself he would have been superhuman if, after staying in their house as he had for so long, he had been able to imagine for one instant they were other than what they appeared to be.

Yet when he came downstairs, he must have seen her mother's portrait in the Study and while she had been exceedingly beautiful, he should have recognised there was at the same time an aristocratic look about her features.

Then Rowena laughed. It was a sound without any humour in it.

She had the same features – she in fact had the same look – in fact they all had!

But the Marquis had not recognised it because it had not been written down in the family tree they did not possess! Where Genealogy was concerned it was not instinct or feelings which counted, but hard facts.

'I hate him! I hate him!' she told herself.

Then remembering how magnificent he had looked that night with his decorations on his breast, she thought despairingly that whatever she said or did his image was engraved on her heart for all time.

·   ·   ·   ·   ·

Driving in the Earl's carriage out of London Rowena calculated that if, as she had instructed him, the coachman put her down at the cross-roads which led to Little Powick, she would be able to leave her trunk in one of the adjacent cottages and walk home in under twenty minutes.

She would be back in the house by four o'clock, and she was quite certain that not only would her father still be out on his round but Hermione and Mark would not yet have returned from their lessons.

This meant that she would be able to change into her ordinary clothes.

It would be fatal for them to see her as she was now arrayed in one of the beautiful afternoon gowns which her grandfather had given her and wearing a chip-straw bonnet trimmed with flowers that had Bond Street written all over it.

She had not liked to disappoint her grandfather by refusing to wear a gown he had given her when she said goodbye.

He had been so kind and so generous that she wished in the short time she was with him to do everything to please him.

She knew that he was thinking that she looked like her mother as she kissed his cheek in the hall and he saw her into his carriage.

"I should really return by Stage-coach," she said.

"I will not have you travelling alone in a public conveyance," he retorted almost fiercely.

Rowena had given in without argument, but she realised that it created problems that she would somehow have to overcome.

It was very difficult, she thought, to avoid hurting her grandfather, without at the same time, hurting her father.

There was no doubt that the Earl still deeply resented the man who had taken his daughter from him, and there was nothing that Rowena could say or do which could make the hurt seem any less.

But though she felt she ought not to accept any clothes from the Earl other than the gown she had required to go to Carlton House, she had not been able to refuse when he had chosen for her several other dresses and two extremely alluring bonnets.

'I will share them with Hermione,' she thought.

Thinking it over she decided that if she wore them occasionally and without any fuss her father probably would not even be aware that she looked different.

It was impossible however, not to feel a very feminine thrill at being for the first time in her life well-dressed.

It was exciting too to travel in the Earl's comfortable, if slightly old-fashioned, carriage drawn by four well-bred horses.

They were not in any way the equal of those owned by the Marquis, any more than the elderly grey-haired coachman resembled Sam, but to Rowena they represented the height of luxury.

Having left Dunvegan House she sat back to enjoy the drive and savour for the moment the feeling not only of being rich, but also of being dressed as became a Lady of Quality.

'No-one in the village,' she thought, 'would ever believe where I was last night.'

She knew it would be difficult not to tell Hermione all about the Carlton House fête and describe to her the gowns and jewels of the Regent's guests and, of course, the Regent himself.

He had been even fatter than she had expected from the descriptions she had read in the newspapers and the cartoons she had seen from time to time.

But he had an undeniable charm and she realised as she watched him at the supper-table that he was extremely intelligent and that even the most distinguished guests present were hanging on his words.

'I can understand the Marquis liking him, and wishing to be in his company,' she thought.

Then she told herself that what the Marquis liked or did not like was no concern of hers, and the sooner she stopped thinking about him so often the better.

The carriage was soon out of the city and now they were on the dusty lanes over which Rowena had travelled so slowly in the Stage-coach.

She calculated now they would reach the cross-roads earlier than she expected and she hoped that there would be few people to see her as she hurried through the village.

'They will certainly think me very smart,' she thought.

Then she remembered that at this time of the day the men and women were in the fields helping with the harvest.

There would doubtless be only the very old and half-blind and a number of children about.

'I am worrying quite unnecessarily,' Rowena told herself.

But she knew she had no wish that anyone should ask where she had been or why she had arrived home in such an unusual manner.

The horses were travelling fast and Rowena found herself wishing that she could sit beside the coachman on the box.

She had always hated being shut up inside a carriage and although she had been so worried and so anxious about Mark it had been an experience she would never forget to drive with the Marquis in the Phaeton behind his magnificent team of chestnuts.

Suddenly and unexpectedly the horses were drawn in sharply and the carriage came to a standstill.

"What has happened? What is the matter?" Rowena called out.

The thought of highwaymen flashed through her mind.

She realised the coachman was shouting in a somewhat hoarse voice and she bent forward to look out of the window. As she did so she gave a gasp.

Standing across the road so that it was impossible to pass was a Phaeton she recognised, drawn by four horses.

They were moving restlessly backwards and forwards.

138

A groom was running towards her carriage and when she realised that it was Sam she sat back quickly on the seat, feeling her heart beating tempestuously.

"What be it? Why be ye a-holding us up?" she heard the old coachman ask.

"I've a message for Miss Winsford."

Sam came to the window of the carriage.

"His Lordship asks, Miss, if you'll transfer immediately to his Phaeton. Sommat has happened of th' utmost importance."

'What is it?" Rowena asked. "An accident?"

"His Lordship didn't say, Miss. He only asks if you'll come quick-like."

Rowena looked at Sam and asked:

"What is it, Sam? You must know."

Then despite herself she gave a little cry.

"It is not .. Master Mark?"

"I don't know, Miss and that's the truth," Sam replied, "but His Lordship wouldn't say 'tis important if t'aint."

"What can have occurred?"

They were by now near to Little Powick and it seemed pointless to argue when the Marquis could easily follow her to the cross-roads and pick her up when the carriage left her there.

At the same time she was exceedingly reluctant to do as he wished unless it was something which concerned the family . . .

She had a sudden feeling of fear that her father might have been in an accident.

Suppose he had been involved in the same type of collision which had injured the Marquis?

"I will come and speak to His Lordship," she said, making up her mind.

Sam opened the door of the carriage and she stepped out on the road.

As she walked towards the Marquis she heard Sam ask the footman to help him with her trunk.

She reached the Phaeton and looked up at the Marquis who seemed very high above her.

"What has happened? Has there been an accident?"

Although she tried to speak coldly she could not help the note of agitation creeping into her voice.

"Get in and I will tell you," he replied.

For a moment Rowena hesitated, then she realised that Sam and the footman were just behind her.

Tentatively, because there seemed to be nothing else she could do, she put one foot on the step and the Marquis stretched out his hand.

Although she had no wish to take it she needed his assistance to climb up into the seat beside him.

She sat down and as she did so the Marquis took a guinea from his pocket and threw it down to the Earl's footman who had deposited her trunk at the back of the Phaeton.

He caught the gold coin, grinned and touched the brim of his hat.

"Thank ye, M'Lord."

The Marquis drew his horses back into the centre of the road and they moved off.

It all happened so quickly that Rowena realised that she had not thanked her grandfather's servants and in fact even now did not understand why she had been persuaded to change vehicles.

"Where are we going?" she asked after a moment as the Marquis did not speak.

He made no reply and she said:

"I insist on your telling me why you stopped me in this extraordinary manner. If it is bad news, I would rather hear it at once than frighten myself into imagining things which may not necessarily have happened."

"Let me set your mind at rest by telling you there has been no accident."

"Then you have no right to stop me in this ridiculous way."

"I think I have every right!"

There was something in the way he spoke which made Rowena look at him suspiciously. She thought as she glanced at his profile that his chin was firm and perhaps even more aggressive than usual.

It certainly seemed very square above the whiteness of his intricately tied cravat and she imagined too, that his mouth was specially firm.

"I thought you realised last night that I had no wish to see you again," she said.

"You made your feelings perfectly clear."

"Then why not do as I ask and leave me alone?"

"That is unfortunately something I am unable to do."

"If this is just another trick to try to force me into doing what you wish, I shall be exceedingly angry."

The Marquis appeared to be intent on his driving and after a moment she went on:

"I have asked my grandfather to speak to you, which I think he intended to do some time this afternoon. He understands the whole situation and agrees that in the circumstances there is no point in your seeing me again or having anything to do with my family."

"Your grandfather intends to take you all under his wing?"

That was a question Rowena could not answer with any satisfaction.

She thought bitterly that the Marquis was well aware that her grandfather could do nothing for her or the children without it being an intolerable insult to her father.

"My grandfather's intentions can be of no interest to you," she managed to say, "and I want an answer, My Lord, as to why you are here and where you are taking me. I have to be home by four o'clock."

"I am afraid you will be late," the Marquis answered.

"But .. why?"

Then as Rowena asked the question she realised they had reached a turning which led not towards Little Powick but directly to Swayneling Park.

"Where are we going?" she asked quickly. "I have told you that I have to be home before four, and I insist you turn your horses immediately and take me there."

"And if I do not obey you?" the Marquis asked.

She looked at him uncertainly out of the corner of her eyes.

The only alternative she could think of was to jump out of the Phaeton. That not only would be very undignified, but she would certainly hurt herself. What was more, the Marquis would doubtless merely pick her up again and carry on as he intended.

Rowena bit her lip with vexation and felt her temper rising.

Whatever she did she seemed to come up against the Marquis in a way that made her feel small and ineffectual.

She had planned last night to defy him in a manner which would make him humble and apologetic, instead of which he seemed more overwhelming and more awe-inspiring than ever.

She thought he was looking grim and rather stern, but that was not the expression she wanted to see on his face.

It was also, although she hated to admit it, somewhat intimidating.

She relapsed into silence and they drove on until suddenly there in front of them were the huge stone-flanked wrought-iron gates of Swayneling Park.

The Marquis turned in at them, and now a thousand thoughts flashed through Rowena's mind as to what his intentions were in taking her to his house.

Did he mean to impress her as she had been impressed when she had journeyed down the same drive in Edward Lawson's chaise?

Or was there a stranger and perhaps more sinister reason that she could not fathom?

Then as she saw the great house, exquisite in the afternoon sunshine, the windows flashing iridescent in front of them, the Marquis turned to the left.

Nestling among the trees in the Park there was a small grey Church which Rowena had not noticed on her previous visit.

It was not far from the main drive down a narrow roadway to the lych-gate which opened into a small church-yard filled with ancient tombstones.

The Marquis drew his horses to a standstill and Sam ran to their heads. Then the Marquis threw down the reins and began to take off his driving-gloves.

As he did so he turned to look at Rowena.

Her eyes were very large in her small face.

"Why have you brought me here?" she asked, and her voice was hardly above a whisper.

"To marry you!" the Marquis replied.

CHAPTER SEVEN

For a moment it was impossible to speak. Then Rowena replied:

"I will never marry you! Nothing you can say or do will . . make me!"

She thought the Marquis's expression did not change and he answered quietly:

"There is of course an alternative."

"What is . . that?"

"If you refuse to marry me, I will take you to my house and keep you there for a week. I shall then notify your father and your grandfather where you are, and I think you will find that they will both do their best to persuade you to become my wife."

At first Rowena could hardly understand what he was saying. Then she gasped.

"You . . cannot do . . that to . . me!"

"I can and I will!" the Marquis replied firmly.

She met his eyes defiantly. Then she felt that while he looked grim and was saying one thing, his eyes were saying something very different.

Despite herself, despite every resolution not to be moved by him, she felt her heart begin to beat frantically in a manner she knew so well.

"The choice is yours," the Marquis said. "It has to be one or the other."

Desperately Rowena tried to think of another solution.

She could try to run away, but the Marquis would easily catch her and she would appear very undignified in front of Sam.

She knew too, that if he took her to Swayneling Park there would be no escape.

The servants would obey him, and moreover in some secret part of herself she knew that if she was alone with the Marquis for a week she would find it very difficult to refuse what he wanted of her whether she was married or not.

'I love him!' she thought despairingly, 'and yet at the same time I hate him for what he has done to me!'

The horses moved uneasily and it was as if they, rather than the Marquis made up Rowena's mind.

"I will .. marry .. you," she said in a voice that was hardly audible.

"I thought you would see sense," he replied.

He climbed down from the Phaeton and lifted Rowena to the ground.

She thought he might hold her for a moment against him, but his hands only held her waist. Then after he had opened the lych-gate and she passed through it he offered her his arm.

She felt as if she moved in a dream and that what was happening could not be true. Yet they walked along the short pathway to the Church porch and without pausing passed through it into the aisle.

The Church was small, quiet, cool and dim.

There were six candles burning on the altar, an old Priest in a white surplice was waiting for them and there was the fragrance of lilies.

The Marquis's firm footsteps seemed to echo as he walked up the aisle, while Rowena's in contrast seemed light and somehow hesitant.

When they reached the altar steps, the Clergyman opened his book and began the Service.

Rowena had taken her hand from the Marquis's arm and she felt somehow alone and separated from him until the moment when he took her fingers in his.

Then she felt a little quiver run through her and his voice sounded very grave and serious as he repeated the well-known words:

"To have and to hold from this day forward, for better, for worse, for richer, for poorer, in sickness and in health, to love and to cherish, till death us do part."

'This is what I always wanted,' she told herself.

Yet she knew there was a shadow on her happiness that could never be erased.

It was only because of her grandfather they were being married, and if she had not turned to him for protection the Marquis would have remained resolute in his decision that he would not ask her to be his wife.

She felt the ring encircle her finger.

She wondered how the Marquis had known it would fit her. Then they were kneeling side by side and the old Priest was blessing them.

"May God the Father, God the Son, God the Holy Ghost, Bless, preserve and keep you . . ."

Without really meaning to Rowena had slipped her hand into the Marquis's and she felt his fingers tighten on hers.

They were married. She belonged to him and now there was no looking back, no escape.

She shut her eyes to pray that despite everything they would be happy and that he would love her as she loved him – not as much, that would be impossible, but at least there might be some of the glory and rapture left which she had felt when he had first kissed her.

He helped her to her feet, and she found that the Clergyman had gone and they were alone in the quiet little Church.

She looked up at him and felt there was a look of triumph in his eyes, and another expression that she did not understand.

She looked away from him and he took her hand to slip it through his arm so that he could take her down the aisle.

There was only silence in the Church, and yet Rowena felt she heard music – music which came from their hearts and joined with the voices of angels.

The Marquis helped her into the Phaeton and the horses, anxious to reach their stables which they sensed were near, set off at a sharp pace.

There was no chance of speaking and indeed Rowena felt she had nothing to say.

It all seemed unreal: something which had happened in her imagination rather than in fact.

The Marquis drew up with a flourish at the front door and the servants were already there waiting.

"May I congratulate Your Lordship and wish Her Ladyship every happiness," the Butler said.

"Thank you, Newman," the Marquis replied.

"Rowena," he said addressing her for the first time since they had left the Church, "this is Newman who has been with my family for over thirty years. I could not possibly do without him."

Rowena held out her hand.

"All the staff wish to welcome you to Swayneling Park, M'Lady."

"Thank you."

"Her Ladyship is tired," the Marquis said. "We were up late last night and she has had a long journey from London. If Mrs. Mayfield is waiting to look after her, I think she should rest until dinner-time."

"Mrs. Mayfield is at the top of the stairs, M'Lord," Newman answered.

The Marquis escorted Rowena to the foot of them.

"I suggest you have some sleep," he said. "We will not dine until eight, which will give you plenty of time."

He took her hand and raised it to his lips. Rowena had a sudden impulse to hold on to him and say she did not wish to be alone with Mrs. Mayfield or anyone else, but to stay with him.

She felt very shy and lost, and unable to keep up with the swift passage of events.

But obediently, because he expected it of her, she walked up the wide staircase to where waiting at the top landing was an elderly Housekeeper dressed in black with the chatelaine hanging from her waist.

She curtsied, saying as she did so:

"This is a very happy day for all of us, M'Lady. We've wished for a long time that His Lordship would bring home a mistress for Swayneling Park."

•   •   •   •   •

Rowena awoke to find surprisingly that she had slept for a long time, and dreamlessly.

She had in fact felt tired, not because she had been late the night before, but because of all the conflicting emotions she had felt during the day.

She had known when spending the morning with her grandfather that there was a bond between them that she had not expected, and that however difficult it might be she would like to see him again.

It was as if he was a close link with her mother and there was some affinity between them that she could not find with anyone else.

But she knew she had to leave him. He would pass out of her life and become only a memory of brief kindness and generosity.

The feelings that the Marquis had evoked in her were very different.

While she still resented fiercely and rebelliously the manner in which he had forced her to marry him, she could not repress a secret joy in knowing she was his wife.

She had cried so despairingly and yearned for him with every nerve in her body, until now that they were actually married it seemed impossible to believe all the frustration and uncertainty was past.

Yet, as she had thought in the Church, the shadow over their happiness was still there.

'However much he might have wanted me just for myself,' she thought as she lay in the great room to which Mrs. Mayfield had taken her, 'it was not enough.'

The housemaids were bringing in a bath-tub of silver and setting it down on the hearth-rug.

Rowena looked up at the exquisitely painted ceiling depicting Venus surrounded by cupids.

She looked at the carved and gilded furniture, made she was sure in the reign of Charles II, which was also resplendent with cupids.

She realised the bed in which she was lying was very large and draped with silk curtains of Nile blue, embroidered with love-knots.

She blushed a little at the thought of what everything around her portended.

Then realising her bath was ready, she stepped from the bed to bathe in water scented with lilies-of-the-valley.

As she dressed she could not help being glad that she could wear again the beautiful gown which her grandfather had given her last night for the fête at Carlton House.

Amidst all the splendour that surrounded the Marquis, she felt it would be easy for him to crush and over-ride her if she did not feel a little more sure of herself because she was well gowned.

When she was dressed she looked at herself in the mirror and knew that while she had been pretty enough for the Regent to admire last night, this evening she looked different.

Her eyes were very large in her small face and yet there was an apprehensive look in them.

It was fear of the unknown, she thought, and she was a little afraid of the Marquis.

He had always seemed overpowering, and he was even more so now that he was her husband.

Yet she longed for him to admire her. Last night a collet of diamonds had encircled her throat, and she thought that to-night without it she looked a little unfinished.

"It's a very lovely gown, M'Lady," the Housekeeper said behind her, "and very fitting for a bride."

She paused, then she added:

"We always expected His Lordship would bring home someone beautiful, but not as beautiful as you, M'Lady!"

Her words seemed to give Rowena a confidence she needed.

She smiled her thanks, then with her chin held high she walked slowly down the stairs.

Newman was waiting for her in the Hall and he went ahead to open the door to what Rowena knew was the Salon.

It was the loveliest room she had ever seen, with six long windows opening on to a terrace.

The evening sun, gold with a touch of red, seemed to illuminate the room more brightly than the chandeliers could have done and it was in a rosy haze that Rowena saw the Marquis standing at the far end of it.

He was as resplendent as he had been the night before, except that he wore no decorations.

She moved towards him forcing herself to walk slowly although she longed to run.

She wanted to be beside him, she wanted above everything for him to touch her and reassure her, to tell her that what had happened was real and they were together as she had always longed for them to be.

"You look very lovely!"

There was a note in the Marquis's voice which brought the colour to her cheeks. Then he said:

"Last night you wore jewels which I had not given you. That is something which will never happen again. Let me give you my wedding-present."

She saw then that he had a box in his hand, but he did not give it to her. Instead he said:

"I will put it on for you."

She looked in the mirror over the mantelshelf and in it she saw him move behind her. Then something flashed and sparkled as he lifted it in his hands and put it round her neck to fasten it at the back.

For a moment she was so dazzled by it that it was hard to see it distinctly. Then she saw that it was a magnificent necklace of diamonds fashioned in the semblance of flowers.

It was very light but exquisitely beautiful, and in the centre of each flower was a huge blue-white diamond.

She felt the Marquis was waiting for her to speak and after a moment she managed to say:

"It .. is exquisite! Thank you .. very much!"

"I have something else for you," he said, "something I hope you will always wear, even though we somehow omitted the formality of becoming engaged."

He took her left hand as he spoke and slipped on to her third finger a large diamond encircled with smaller ones.

It was so large that it made her hand seem very fragile and as she stared at it, bewildered at possessing anything so valuable, the door opened.

"Dinner is served, M'Lady!"

Rowena realised that she had not thanked the Marquis for this present which was a very personal one. She wondered as they walked towards the Dining-Room whether she might have kissed him had the Butler not interrupted them.

The Dining-Room was small which rather surprised her, until she learnt it was not the great Baronial Hall which was used when they had visitors, but a small room exclusively for their own use.

The table was decorated with white flowers and several pieces of gold plate which Rowena knew without asking must have been in the family for generations.

She could not help feeling that, if she had not been aware of her relationship to the Earl of Dunvegan, she would in fact have felt hopelessly insignificant because everything in this house was a reminder of the Marquis's noble ancestry.

She had not missed the family portraits along the passage or several which hung in the Salon.

Everywhere she looked, she thought, she could feel the eyes of earlier Swaynes following her.

Even the crests on the silver seemed to proclaim the centuries in which they had carried such an emblem on their own persons, on the livery of their servants, on their swords and flags when they went into battle.

Despite the fact that at first she felt she was too emotional to eat the delicious dishes that were brought one after the other to the table, they were hard to resist.

There was champagne to fill the crystal glasses engraved with the Marquis's monogram, and when the servants left the room after the dessert had been served he raised his glass.

"I want to drink a toast to my wife," he said in his deep voice, "and I want you to join me in one to our future happiness."

Rowena picked up her glass.

"I hope I .. shall make you .. happy."

There was just a little doubt behind the words.

She was thinking how different this evening might have been if it had happened a week ago, before she went to London to confront the Marquis at Carlton House and, as she hoped, defeat him.

As if perceptively he knew what was in her mind the Marquis put down his glass and pushed back his chair.

"I have something to show you."

"You do not wish me to leave you to your port?" Rowena asked.

He shook his head.

"I have no wish for you to leave me now or ever."

She did not answer him but rose from her chair and he opened the door for her to leave the Dining-Room.

She would have turned right which she knew was the direction of the Salon; but to her surprise the Marquis guided her towards the left and they walked along a wide corridor, moving, Rowena realised, away from the centre of the house towards the left wing.

There were still more family portraits hanging above carved tables, French commodes and ancient chests, and occasionally a flag which a Swayne must have captured in battle or a sword which Rowena knew would have a history.

At last after they had walked for some way the Marquis stopped to open a door.

Rowena entered a room and thought at first glance it was

an office. Then she saw there were two men in it who rose to their feet as they entered.

Hanging on the walls were many framed manuscripts like those the Marquis had brought to show Hermione of his family tree.

"Good-evening, Mr. Smythson," the Marquis said to the first man standing near the door.

"Good-evening, M'Lord."

"I want you to show Her Ladyship how far you have advanced with the task I set you."

"It will be a pleasure!" Mr. Smythson replied. "And as it happens, M'Lord, it has been far easier than I anticipated."

"Mr. Smythson has been researching into the family tree of the Winsfords," the Marquis explained.

Rowena said in some surprise:

"I am not surprised it did not take very long!"

"I have traced the Winsfords in Huntingdon," Mr. Smythson said eagerly, "where His Lordship told me your Ladyship's family lived, back to 1587!"

Rowena stared at him in astonishment.

Then she looked down at the rough design on which he was working and saw in fact that from her father at the foot of it the Winsfords went back one by one until they reached Richard Winsford at the date Mr. Smythson had given her.

"I had no idea this was possible!" she exclaimed.

"I thought it would surprise you," the Marquis said, "and Mr. Smythson has not finished yet. There is a great deal more research he can do."

"Yes, indeed, M'Lord," Mr. Smythson agreed. "I have several men making investigations amongst the Libraries, the County Records and other sources which should provide us with new and I think, extremely interesting material."

He paused to say to Rowena:

"I am afraid, Your Ladyship, I can't trace the maiden name of your mother."

Rowena glanced at the Marquis.

"I will let you have all their particulars tomorrow, Mr. Smythson," the Marquis replied.

As he spoke he drew Rowena to the other end of the room.

"This is Mr. Gaylord," he said, "who has been working with me for many years. The way he illustrates and illuminates is in the tradition of the ancient manuscripts I showed you."

"Thank you M'Lord," Mr. Gaylord smiled.

"This is what Mr. Gaylord is working on now," the Marquis said, "my family tree. As it is a very long one it has to be spread out."

On a long oak table in front of the window Rowena saw a parchment which must have been nearly six feet in length.

She realised that it was beautifully illuminated with miniatures and historiated initials exactly like the medieval ones.

"It starts, M'Lady," Mr. Gaylord explained, "with Comte Etienne de Swayne, whose grandson was in the army of William the Conqueror when he left Normandy for these shores."

He pointed to the name as he spoke at the top of the tree. Then he moved slowly, passing from the Norman Swaynes to the Medieval ones, from the Tudor to the Hanoverians, and finally Rowena following his pointing finger found the Marquis's name at the very bottom of the parchment.

She saw his full name as she had heard it last in the Church as they were married: "Tarquin Alexander, 5th Marquis of Swayne."

And there beside it was – her own name! "Rowena Mary Winsford."

"I want you to tell Her Ladyship the date on which I instructed you, Mr. Gaylord, to add her name to this tree," the Marquis said. "I am sure you can remember it exactly."

"Of course, M'Lord," Mr. Gaylord replied. "It was three days ago on July 30th, the night before you left for London."

Rowena was very still.

"You are quite certain that you remember my coming to

this room on that day to give you that instruction?" the Marquis asked.

"Quite certain, M'Lord!" Mr. Gaylord answered in a puzzled tone. "It is not a date I am likely to forget, considering how delighted we were that Your Lordship was to be married."

"Thank you, Mr. Gaylord."

The Marquis took Rowena by the arm and drew her from the room.

As they walked silently down the long corridor she found she was holding her breath.

He had intended to marry her before he knew about her grandfather! He had changed his mind, and yet he had not told her so but had gone away, leaving her thinking that she was not good enough for him and that blood was more important than love.

They entered the Salon and the Marquis closed the door behind him.

Then as Rowena walked to the fireplace he went to the window to stand as he had done the night they had kissed, with his back towards her, looking out into the garden.

She felt as if the silence vibrated between them. Then at last when she felt as if no words would come to her lips the Marquis said:

"I have won, but after all it is a hollow victory."

Rowena stiffened.

It flashed through her mind that what he was saying was that now she was his wife he was regretting it and no longer wanted her.

"When I kissed you," he went on, "I told you I felt as if I had found a new, unlisted flower on top of a mountain. What we felt for each other was so perfect, so incredible that now I am afraid."

"W . why?"

Rowena's voice sounded strange even to herself.

"Because through my own stupidity I have trampled on that flower and may have destroyed it."

There was silence, then Rowena said tremulously:

"W . why did you . . not tell me?"

"There did not seem to be an opportunity when you were so glad to have found Mark, and I knew your thoughts were only of him," the Marquis answered. "Also I knew I had to go to London. I could not refuse to be in attendance on the Regent when he had expressly asked for me."

He paused a moment before he continued:

"But I meant to come back to you to-day and ask you formally and with due ceremony if you would honour me by becoming my wife."

"I had no . . idea that you had . . changed your . . mind," Rowena murmured.

"It is difficult to explain what I felt when I told you that I could not offer you marriage," the Marquis said. "I suppose the truth is that I had never known love – real love before. It took me unawares and, although it was the most perfect thing that had ever happened to me, I could not for the moment reconcile it with the conventions that had been part of my upbringing, my innermost thoughts, and my whole life."

"And yet . . you changed . . your mind."

"It was Mark who did that."

"Mark?"

"When I realised how anxious you were about him on the Newmarket Road, when you thought we had gone the wrong way, I suddenly knew I wanted my wife to feel like that if she had lost our own child – your son and mine, Rowena."

He paused.

"I had been so precise and perhaps, if you like, so obstinate in planning my future that I had not considered that children need love, a love that is a part of their family life, a love which their mother and their father have for each other."

The Marquis gave a deep sigh.

"I think in that moment I realised why you were all so

beautiful, why you and your whole family had such fine and noble characters, and why Mark was so brave. He has not only a horsemanship which I admire, but an independence which I would like my own son to have."

There was a note in the Marquis's eyes that made the tears prick Rowena's.

He was in fact expressing in words what she had felt herself that as a family they had always been encompassed with love because their father and mother had loved each other so deeply.

"I came back here after I had left you," the Marquis continued, "and I went straight to Mr. Gaylord and told him to add your name to the family tree. The only thing that was missing was the date of our marriage, and that I was determined should take place as soon as possible after I returned."

"If only .. you could have .. told me," Rowena murmured.

She thought how miserable she had been, how deeply she had resented him, and how with the help of her grandfather she had tried to cast him out of her life.

"I realised at Carlton House that I had made a mess of everything," the Marquis said in a low voice, "and because I knew exactly what you were thinking and feeling, my darling, as I always have, I was desperately frightened that I might lose you completely. That was why I came back here very early this morning from London and arranged our marriage."

Rowena did not speak and after a moment he said with a different note in his voice:

"I was afraid – terribly afraid, – that your grandfather might persuade you to go to Scotland with him, or that you would really manage somehow, my precious, to keep me out of your home."

"It would have been .. difficult to do .. that."

"How could I be certain? How could I be sure of anything except that I wanted you? As I want you now."

Again there was silence until the Marquis said aloud:

"Have I lost your love?"

Because she was so deeply attuned to everything he said, Rowena knew there was an agony behind the words.

He was feeling, she thought, as she had felt when she learnt that his love for her was not the love she had sought and longed for.

Because she loved him so overwhelmingly she could not bear him to be unhappy and apprehensive.

Yet for a moment she felt too shy to move, too shy to speak.

Then she moved until when she spoke again she was just behind him. But he was still looking into the garden.

"If .. you kissed me," she whispered in a voice he could only just hear, "perhaps we would .. know if our love is .. still there and still .. as wonderful as it was .. before."

He turned round and she saw the light in his eyes as if it came from a flame in his heart.

"Do you mean that?" he asked. "Oh, my darling! Do you really mean it?"

Her eyes looked up into his and there was no need to answer.

Her lips were soft and waiting for him.

She was not certain if he pulled her to him or if she moved first, but his arms went round her to hold her very close.

In the golden light from the setting sun he looked down into her face for a long moment, then his mouth came down on hers.

Just for one flashing second she was afraid that the magic and enchantment had gone.

Then even more rapturous, more wonderful, more glorious than it had been before, there was the warm wave moving up through her throat to her lips.

A streak of lightning flashed through her body which was half pain, half glory and a part of the Divine.

It was everything she had longed for and thought she had lost for ever.

In a way it was even more marvellous because she had passed through so much suffering, as he had.

"My little love! My beautiful one!" the Marquis cried. "You are everything that is perfect, everything I have longed for and everything I so nearly lost!"

His voice was unsteady and Rowena's as she answered him was tremulous with the emotions he had aroused in her.

"I .. love you!" she whispered. "I love you .. more than I have .. ever loved you before!"

"Do you mean that? You forgive me?"

"There is .. nothing to forgive. Mama said that when I found the man I truly .. loved it would be destiny and there was nothing I could do about it."

The Marquis's arms tightened about her and he drew her closer.

"It was fate that brought us to each other but we duelled with destiny and that was unforgivable. I might have lost you!"

Rowena heard again the pain in his voice.

"We have .. found each other .. now."

"I shall thank God for it all my life," the Marquis said. "You are so precious, my adorable little wife, that I will never take risks again for fear I might lose you."

"You will .. never do .. that," Rowena answered.

She knew now that she could never really have resisted him for long.

She was a part of him as she had been since the first moment he kissed her, in fact before that, when she had first seen him lying unconscious on a gate outside the front door.

There were so many things she wanted to say to him, so many things they could talk over together, there was so much she had to learn.

But all she wanted now was to be safe in his arms and feel that incredible rapture when his lips touched hers.

Because she needed him so desperately she stood on tip-toe so that her mouth was nearer to his.

"I .. love .. you!" she whispered.

"Say it again," he ordered. "I want to be certain it is the truth."

"I .. love you."

"For ever?"

"For .. ever."

"And you trust me?"

"You know .. I do."

"You are mine — mine and I will hold you and keep you with me by day and night! I can never lose you again."

"You will .. not do .. that!"

"You are sure?"

"Completely .. and utterly .. sure."

Again he looked down at her as if he must impress her beauty forever on his mind.

Then his lips were on hers holding her completely captive, making her, as he had intended to do, his own.

While she knew that he would always be her master and she would always be subservient to him, she gloried in his strength, his determination and even his obstinacy.

Whatever he was like he was hers, and she was his.

It was destiny, and they neither of them had any defence against it.

THE END